A Plague Doctor Adventure

The Incident at Linwood Mall

By Christopher Tupa

Ctupa.com

Copyright 2021 by Christopher Tupa. All rights reserved.

Content relating to the SCP Foundation, including the SCP Foundation logo,is licensed under Creative Commons Sharealike 3.0 and all concepts originate from http://www.scp-wiki.net and its authors.This artwork, being derived from this content, is hereby also released under Creative Commons Sharealike 3.0.

Prologue

BEEP - BEEP - BEEP

The constant repetitive beeping of an alarm sounded throughout all twelve floors of the SCP Foundation building. The white fluorescent lights hanging from the ceiling every six feet were switched off and red alert lights were flashing instead.

The corridor was lined with solid steel doors, all of which were slowly sliding open.

One of the doors, with the number *049* stamped on it, slid all the way open, revealing a dark room beyond. The only light inside the room was coming from the flashing red light in the hallway.

After a few seconds the long pointy nose of a mask slowly appeared, extending out of the darkness. It was followed by the entire form of the Plague Doctor as he gradually emerged from the room, like a ship sailing through heavy fog.

The doctor wore a black shirt, black pants and a heavy black hooded cloak. To complete the ensemble he wore black leather gloves and boots. Somewhere inside his cloak he carried a medical bag with surgical tools. He carried the bag with him at all times, *always*.

The Plague Doctor stepped out of the dark room and stood in the middle of the empty hallway.

He tilted his head back slightly and took a deep breath.

The doctor looked to the left, then he looked to the right.

After a moment the doctor turned back to the left and began walking briskly down the corridor.

As he walked past the other open rooms, eyes within watched him pass. Nothing else came out of the rooms until *after* the doctor had passed.

The corridor intersected with another corridor, forming a T shape. As the doctor approached the intersection, a scientist wearing a blood stained white lab coat came running around the corner. The scientist was sweating and looking behind him as he ran, and didn't see the Plague Doctor walking towards him until it was too late.

"**Aaghhh!**" screamed the scientist, with panic filled eyes, as he collided with the Plague Doctor. The doctor reached out to stop the scientist as he crashed into him. The scientist looked at the doctor with horror as the doctor grabbed him and they both fell to the ground. The scientist let out another scream as they were falling, but by the time the two hit the floor with a loud thump, the scientist was dead.

As everyone inside the building knows, for reasons unknown to science, any living creature that touches the Plague Doctor *dies*.

The Plague Doctor stood up and dusted off his cloak. He looked down at the dead scientist, bathed in red light, and with a polite nod said, "Ah, my fortunate man, I am a trifle envious of you, now free from this life you may begin your next great adventure."

The doctor then turned and continued walking towards the intersection of the two corridors. He went down the left corridor, walking with purpose, staring straight ahead and never veering from his path. He began to whistle to himself as he made his way through the building.

A great big hairy beast appeared at the end of the hallway and ran towards the doctor. It resembled a large dog, except for the glowing green eyes and pointy horns protruding from it's head. The Plague Doctor continued walking, holding his hands out in front of himself. As the beast neared the doctor it snorted at him but ran around the Plague Doctor, making sure he didn't touch the doctor as he passed.

The Plague Doctor walked on, surrounded by flashing red lights and ringing alarms.

Up in front of the doctor, two scientists ran out of a doorway on the right side of the hall. When they spotted the doctor they both let out screams; turned, and ran back into the room they had come out of, slamming the door behind them. As he passed, the doctor could hear loud scraping noises and the sounds of large objects being piled up behind the door.

The doctor ignored them and continued to walk quickly and steadily down the corridor.

A man wearing black military gear emerged from a door at the end of the hallway. His pants were torn and covered in blood, he had no helmet on, and there were no weapons in his hands. He was panting hard and looked very frightened as he leaned against the door, catching his breath.

The Plague Doctor stopped whistling and stood still, watching the soldier. The soldier hadn't yet noticed the doctor standing in the middle of the hallway. The Plague Doctor turned his head, quizzically studying the uniformed man.

Ah, another soul ready to shake free of their earthy bonds and take that next exciting step into the unknown, the doctor thought happily.

The soldier glanced up and saw the Plague Doctor standing there, unmoving. The man jumped back in shock, banging against the door.

He reached for the pistol strapped to his belt.

The holster was empty.

When the man realized this he froze in fear. Having no weapons to fight the Plague Doctor with, he turned around, opened the door he had just come out of and ran back through. The soldier slammed the door shut and disappeared from sight.

The Plague Doctor shook his head in disappointment and began to walk again. He went through more doors and down more corridors.

Strange and weird creatures passed him in the hallways but they always avoided him, keeping as far away from him as possible.

Any person who saw him turned and ran away; usually screaming as they ran.

The Plague Doctor went up several flights of stairs and walked through more doors and down more corridors.

The alarms continued to sound inside the building and the red lights kept flashing.

The doctor walked on, whistling as he went.

Eventually one of the doors the Plague Doctor opened led outside the building.

It was dark outside; dark and quiet.

The building was surrounded by a shadowy, foreboding forest.

The doctor stepped through the door and disappeared into the pitch black woods.

Chapter 1

The light blue Ford Focus pulled into the huge vacant parking lot surrounding the abandoned Linwood Mall. At one time, over fifteen years ago, this same empty parking lot would have been packed with shoppers. Now, the only thing filling up the acres of concrete is grass and weeds, growing out of numerous cracks in the pavement.
The Ford Focus slowly drove by the front of the mall, passing it's now boarded up main entrance. All the outer stores that had their own entrances to the mall were boarded up as well; the large shoe store, the buffet style restaurant and the appliance store; all empty.
Inside the small car, three people peered through the windows intently, studying the decaying mall as they slowly circled it.
The car went around the corner of the mall and continued to drive down the side, past an old and empty JCPenney store. Then the car, with its three passengers turned another corner and arrived at the backside of the old forgotten mall. The car slowly cruised along the mall perimeter.
Cole was driving the car, and with him were his two best friends; Eddie and Kayla. The three of them were scouting out a location for their next YouTube channel video.
"There!" shouted Eddie, pointing excitedly out the window. "Over by those big green boxes."
Next to the boarded up East Mall entrance was a small alcove set back from the sidewalk. There were several large shrubs and behind those were two huge green metal boxes.
Cole saw what Eddie was pointing at and steered the car in that direction.
"Those are transformers, underground transformers," said Cole as he pulled up next to the large green cabinets.
The three friends looked out the windows, inspecting the green metal boxes Cole said were transformers, and the surrounding area around them.

"Behind them," said Eddie, pointing out the window, "there's a boarded up door. You can barely see it behind the shrubs and transformers. It's well hidden from sight, might be the perfect spot to get inside the mall."

Cole nodded in agreement, "Best option we've seen so far."

"Yes!" said Eddie, clapping his hands together. "This is going to be great!"

"Looks like that's our gateway to adventure boys!" said Kayla with a smile. "We'll come back early tomorrow morning and try it out. I'm sure we'll be able to get in."

Eddie grinned, "Tomorrow it is, tomorrow we explore the *Linwood Mall!*"

"This is going to be one epic video!" said Cole excitedly, as he drove out of the mall parking lot, "*Totally epic!*"

Chapter 2

A dark figure slowly emerged at the edge of the woods.
It stepped closer, stopping so it was just barely concealed by the shade from the trees and surveyed its surroundings. The wooded area ended at a large grassy space, and just beyond that was a paved parking lot that sat in front of a small, brown brick building. On the side of the building in blue letters was a sign that said *Brighton Leadership Academy*.

The figure in the shadows nodded it's head slightly, "Ah...that institution looks like the perfect place to begin my work," it quietly said with satisfaction.
The figure stepped completely out from the woods and into the sunlight.
It was the Plague Doctor.
The doctor took a moment to enjoy the warmth and brightness of the sunlight.
He smiled to himself, pleased with his escape from the SCP facility and his success at having evaded capture thus far.

The doctor picked leaves and small twigs from his cloak as he eyed the academy. When he was satisfied his clothing was clean, the doctor strided towards the Leadership Academy, whistling as he walked.
Everything is working out just wonderfully, the doctor thought with a smile.
When he reached the entrance to the academy, he opened the door and stepped inside without any hesitation.

...

Directly inside the Leadership Academy, just beyond the doors, was a small reception desk where a young man sat behind a computer. He looked up when the doctor entered the building.
"Hello..." he said, staring at the Plague Doctor curiously.

"Greetings to you as well," the doctor responded, pleasantly.
"Can I help you?"
"Yes," the doctor said as he approached the man sitting at the desk. When the doctor was close enough to the man, he stuck his hand out in greeting, "It is indeed a pleasure to meet you."
The man slowly put his hand out as well, "Uhh...you too?" he said cautiously as he took the Plague Doctor's hand and shook it.
Two seconds later the man lay slumped over his desk, dead. He was laying on his keyboard and a continuous stream of letters were being typed across his screen:

Drtttttyfsatydfgiuoshdbfidhvtydfsytfdtysfduyasduyasfdyuasfdyu

The doctor continued inside the building and investigated. He found a storage closet, a large empty classroom, a classroom that he could hear voices emanating from and a pair of restrooms. As the doctor passed by the restrooms, a young woman exited the women's restroom. She saw the doctor and jerked back in surprise, eyeing him warily.
"Hello," said the doctor cheerfully.
The woman nodded at him, "Uh, yeah," she said suspiciously, taking a step backwards.
The doctor suddenly rushed at the woman, she tried to turn and run but the doctor grabbed her wrist before she could get away.
Dead, she fell to the floor with a thump.
The doctor walked back to the occupied classroom and prepared to make his entrance.

. . .

Natalia had been hunched over her desk, in the middle of writing an opening dialogue for a speech on wind turbines when a figure walked into the classroom.
"What-?" she muttered to herself, as she looked up at the strange costumed person standing in the doorway to her classroom. The figure was wearing a black mask with a long nose and a full length black coat with a hood pulled up over its head.

"Think you got the wrong class," smirked Jeff, a student sitting a few rows in front of Natalia. Jeff had been working on a speech about solar powered water wells but stopped to stare at the masked stranger.

Mrs. Jackson, the professor, slowly walked towards the newcomer, "Can I help you?" she asked.

The masked figure slowly turned to address her, "I believe so," he said cheerfully. "You all can."

The stranger sounded polite and sincere but something about the whole scene was making Natalia anxious and edgy. She put her pen down and nervously watched the cloaked figure.

Levi was sitting at the desk closest to the stranger and he stopped working on his assignment and turned in his seat to watch the stranger with a wary eye.

The oddly dressed figure took another step into the classroom.

The air inside the classroom suddenly got very still and tense.

The masked figure reached out and touched Levi on the arm. "Hey!" exclaimed Levi, as he jumped back, slamming into the back of his chair. He then immediately slumped forward, his head landing on the desktop with a loud smack.

Someone beside Natalia let out a scream.

Then someone else screamed.

Kenny, a big guy sitting next to Levi, got up out of his seat and rushed at the cloaked figure, tackling him and knocking him to the ground.

There were more screams.

The masked figure stood up.

Kenny did not.

Another student screamed.

By then most of the students were out of their seats, unsure where to go or what to do. Some of them reached for their phones, but suddenly, without warning, the masked figure, like a blur raced through the room, his hands flying in all directions, touching every single person in the classroom. A few students tried to run around the Plague Doctor and get out of the classroom but the doctor was faster and blocked the doorway.

They never made it out.

Eventually the screams stopped and the room fell silent.

The Plague Doctor looked over the mass of dead bodies laying scattered across the room and slumped over desks.

"Time to get to work," he said gleefully, as he started to whistle.

Chapter 3

"Ready?" asked Cole, pointing his digital camera at Kayla.

"Ok, go," answered Kayla with a nod, then she spoke directly into the camera, "Welcome to another episode of *The Lost Explorers*. I'm Kayla and as usual joining me on today's adventure are Cole and Eddie."

Cole panned the camera around to show Eddie, standing beside Kayla. Eddie stood there with a serious look on his face, trying to look cool as he waved two fingers in a salute. Cole then turned the camera on himself, "Hey!" he said, waving to the camera.

He panned the camera back around to Kayla and she continued, "Today we are going to explore the abandoned Linwood Mall. The Linwood Mall has been officially shut down for eight years but had been slowly dying long before that. In this video, we're going to show you what the inside of the mall looks like today."

Cole stopped recording when Kayla finished talking. "Sounds good," he said. "This would be a good spot to put in some exterior footage of the mall and do a voice over detailing some more of the origins and history of the mall."

"Works for me," said Kayla.

"You guys ready to go in?" asked Eddie, excitedly as he bobbed from side to side.

Kayla smiled, "I've been wanting to check out this mall forever!"

"Me too!" Cole agreed. "This video is going to be sick!"

It was early Friday morning and the trio of urban explorers were standing outside the Linwood Mall by the green transformers they had scoped out the day before. They had driven around the mall three times looking for the best way to get inside and they'd determined the hidden door behind the large green transformers was it. The three friends had a YouTube channel where they documented their urban exploring adventures and the Linwood Mall had been on their list of must see places for a long time. Today they were finally going to sneak in and check it out.

Kayla was wearing old jeans, brown hiking boots and a blue sweatshirt. Eddie was dressed in all black, Eddie was *always* dressed in all black. Cole had tan cargo pants with black combat boots and a long sleeve grey shirt. They each had on a backpack containing cameras, flashlights, extra batteries, snacks, and water bottles. Eddie carried a first aid kit, Kayla had a taser and Cole had pepper spray. They hadn't run into any trouble on their explorations so far, but it didn't hurt to be prepared.

"Let's get inside already!' said Cole energetically as he quickly walked between the huge green transformers and went to the boarded up door tucked away behind them. He examined the boards that were nailed to the door and felt around the edges and corners, looking for a weak spot. The piece of plywood covering the door wasn't secured to all four corners and the bottom right corner was loose enough to pull up on. Cole squatted down by the corner of the door and grabbed the rotten wood and pulled, creating a small space between the wood and the door.

Kayla knelt down next to Cole and looked through the gap, "Glass is busted out," she said, "someone's been here before."

Eddie was standing right behind the two, "Probably why that corner is loose," he said. "Can we get through?"

Kayla unzipped her backpack and took out her flashlight. She turned it on and shone it behind the wood and into the room beyond.

"Looks like it," she said. "Just watch the glass on the other side, it's everywhere."

Cole got a flashlight out of his backpack and prepared to crawl into the room, "Hold the wood for me," he said to Kayla. She pulled back on the wood with both hands, creating a space big enough for Cole to squeeze through. She could hear the crunching of glass as he half-crawled, half-squatted his way through and stood up inside the room.

Kayla leaned down and peered inside the room. She could see the beam of light from Cole's flashlight circling around the room.

"How's it look?" she asked, as Eddie paced anxiously behind her.

"Looks like a basic maintenance room. There's some breaker panels and junky filing cabinets. The floor's a real mess."

"No monsters?" asked Eddie. "No axe murderers?"

"Nope, no monsters. There's only one axe murderer but he's sleeping."

"Funny," said Eddie, "real funny guy."

"Coast is clear, come on in," Cole said as he used the side of his boot to push a lot of the broken glass away from the door.

"Yes!" exclaimed Eddie, still pacing behind Kayla with nervous energy.

Eddie knelt down next to Kayla and held the wood back so she could crawl through. Once she was through she pressed on the plywood from the other side and Eddie squeezed through.

Eddie and Kayla stood up inside the room and Kayla fanned her flashlight around. The floor was covered in dirt, grime and broken glass. There were several puddles of water in the middle of the room. The plaster covering the walls was rotting and falling off, making soggy moldy piles on the floor.

Some of the ceiling tiles were covered in water stains and were sagging and drooping. A great many of the tiles had fallen and were laying on the floor, slowly decomposing.

"This is gross," said Eddie with disgust as he looked around the room. "Lot's of mold in here."

Cole had his camera out and was filming the interior of the room. Kayla was shining her light around at the various slimy puddles and piles of debris littering the floor, "I sure hope the rest of the mall isn't this bad."

Cole had walked to the far side of the room and was standing by a grey metal door, "Only one way to find out," he said, nodding his head towards the door. "Ready?"

"Heck yeah!" Eddie exclaimed as he and Kayla walked over to join him. Eddie was very careful to avoid stepping in any of the sludge covering the floor.

"Here goes," said Cole, as he twisted the handle and opened the door.

Chapter 4

The Plague Doctor stood up and stepped back.
He looked down at his 'patient' lying on the classroom floor and appraised his handiwork.
The doctor smiled.
He had just finished operating on his second dead body; that of a young man in a red t-shirt.
"Arise my friend, arise," commanded the Plague Doctor.
As the doctor watched, the dead man slowly sat up; then with shaking legs he stood all the way up.
"Well done," said the doctor, pleased with his successful operation.
The doctor's strange powers do more than cause death. Although anyone the doctor touches does die, if he operates on the body, they become a zombie totally under his control. Science cannot explain it, and has no explanation for why this happens.
The Plague Doctor pointed to the side of the room, "Now go and join your brother," the doctor instructed his new creation.
The man, now an undead zombie, shambled over to the side of the classroom and joined one other zombie standing along the wall. The other zombie, also a former student of the Leadership Academy, stood staring straight ahead, patiently waiting for the doctors next order.
The Plague Doctor walked over to the closest corpse laying on the floor. He knelt down beside it, and using the medical tools he carries with him, began to operate, just as he had on the previous dead body.
"So much work to be done," the doctor said joyfully. "So much work."

Chapter 5

Cole opened the door.

His flashlight illuminated a long, windowless, white-walled corridor.

"It looks like the end of this hallway opens into the mall," Eddie said eagerly, looking over Cole's shoulder.

Eddie could hardly contain himself and was gently pushing Cole forward, "Go!" he said playfully.

Cole stepped through the door and into the corridor. Eddie and Kayla followed and they all began to walk slowly down the hallway.

The corridor had some water damage and a lot of graffiti but other than that it was in pretty decent shape. Cole led the way, continuing to film as Eddie and Kayla followed right behind him, giddy with excitement.

We're so close! thought Kayla, with a huge grin on her face.

"I can't wait to see this place," said Eddie excitedly. "I hope it's not totally destroyed."

The three friends reached the end of the corridor and stepped out into the mall.

They had made it, they were inside the Linwood Mall.

The three stood there for a second, savoring the thrill of accomplishment.

The mall was eerily quiet.

"Wow," said Kayla looking around at the abandoned and empty mall. "This is *so* neat."

The mall had a lot of skylights that provided an ample amount of natural light, so they switched off their flashlights for the time being.

Around them were empty stores of various sizes and designs. Glass littered the mall floor as well as broken pipes, pieces of wood, and other random bits of trash and material vandals had strewn about.

"Thank goodness it's in better shape than that maintenance room back there," said Eddie, relief evident in his voice. "I can't wait to explore this place!"

Directly across from them was a large store, the front was covered in big pink square tiles, and a sign that said *Shoes*. The first part of the sign had disappeared long ago. The store's glass display windows had been busted and smashed, leaving glass everywhere.

Kayla and Eddie had their phones out and were filming and taking pictures while Cole filmed with his camera.

Cole turned his camera upward and recorded the skylights overhead and the second story balcony above them where a lot of the iron railings and handrails were missing.

"Looks like scrappers have been here," he said, pointing up to where the rails used to be. "We have to be extra careful when we get up there."

Eddie was spinning in a slow circle, looking at the stores around them. As he walked over to one he switched his light back on and shone it inside. "This looks like it was a clothing store," he said, "I can see some metal clothing racks in the back."

The trio slowly walked to the left, exploring the outside of the stores.

"Feels like we're going back in time," said Kayla, gazing at the long forgotten stores with wonder.

Most of the glass windows in the stores had been broken out but every so often there was a store that hadn't been vandalized very much.

The mall floor was covered in a layer of dust. Random papers and moldy cardboard boxes lay scattered along the walls. One of the stores still had some of it's wooden display shelves inside. Yet the store next to it was completely bare, even the ceiling tiles were missing.

The trio passed an overturned customer service kiosk, it's wood counter broken and splintered.

"Hey!" said Cole, pointing to a small space set into the wall on the right side. The walls were covered in white tiles, but there was a large stripe that ran across the middle of the wall made up of small blue and white square ceramic tiles, creating a checkered pattern. "That looks like one of those Auntie Anne pretzel stands the malls used to have!"

"Oh yeah!" said Kayla, snapping a few pics.

"I never did get one but I remember seeing them at like *every* mall *ever!*" said Eddie. "I can almost smell the pretzels."

"I wish," joked Kayla, "all I smell is wet dirt and mold."

Eddie walked over to the center of the mall and looked up at the skylights. He took a few pictures with his phone. He was looking at the upper floor balcony when he noticed something, "Look at all the lightbulbs that used to be here," he said, pointing to the numerous empty light sockets lining the underside of the balcony for as far as they could see. The underside of the entire upper level was lined with empty light sockets.

"Whoa," said Cole, "this place must have been lit up like Vegas back in the day."

"That is a *lot* of light bulbs," Kayla remarked. "I would hate to have to change all those out."

"Maybe that's why they closed the mall," Eddie teased, "they couldn't afford the electric bill for all those lights."

"Check out those colors," said Cole, pointing to two wide stripes painted on the wall directly below the empty light sockets. The top stripe was pink and the bottom stripe was turquoise. The stripes ran underneath the balcony all the way down the length of the mall.

"Now *that* is retro," Kayla said. "That color combination went out of style the same time leg warmers did."

The trio spent a few minutes filming and taking pics of the retro stripes and countless empty light sockets before moving on.

"Man, I love these old malls!" said Eddie. "Brings back some memories. I spent a lot of time in the mall where I grew up."

"Yeah," said Cole, "me too. Never thought I would miss my old mall."

They passed several more empty stores, filming and taking pics of each one.

Kayla suddenly stopped outside an empty store. One of the front windows was busted out, leaving pieces of glass all over the tiled floor. She stepped over the window frame and into the store, "It's Christmas!" she said with a huge smile.

Inside the store, off to one side was a large Christmas tree, complete with lights and ornaments.

"Oh, Wow," said Cole, filming as he too walked into the store and up to the tree.

"Any presents under it?" asked Eddie with a grin, joining the other two as they stood beside the tree.

"No," said Kayla. "There's some rat poop for you though."

She touched a few of the ornaments, "They're glued on," she said, wiping her hands on her jeans, "and covered in dust."

"Didn't expect to see a Christmas tree in here," remarked Cole, as he turned and exited the store. "Wonder what other crazy stuff we'll find in here."

Chapter 6

It had been several hours and the Plague Doctor had created fourteen zombies.

He stood in the center of the classroom surveying his creations. He had instructed the first three zombies he'd made to move the desks out of the room and line all the bodies in rows on the floor. At least twenty bodies still lay on the floor, waiting to be operated on.

The Plague Doctor was thinking.

"My friends," he said, turning to face his zombies as they stood in a line against the far wall, "each of you will pick up a body and follow me, we must relocate to a more suitable location. It is only a matter of time before these people are missed and someone comes looking for them."

His zombies slowly walked over to the dead students and their teacher laying on the floor, and each one of them bent down and picked up a body. The zombies, with their gruesome cargo, lined up behind the doctor who then led the way out of the room.

The Plague Doctor glanced at the bodies they had to leave behind and shook his head with sadness and regret.

"Such a waste, they would have been extremely useful to me."

He then turned and walked out of the classroom. With his zombie servants following him, the doctor walked down a short hallway, past the receptionist lying slumped over his keyboard, and out the front door of the small Leadership Academy building.

The doctor stopped outside the door and scanned the area around the academy. Behind the building and to the left were the woods the doctor had been in last night. To the right of the building, some 500 feet away was the decaying ruins of an old mall; The Linwood Mall.

The doctor studied the large abandoned structure for a moment.

"Ah!" he exclaimed with joy, "That will be the perfect place to continue my work uninterrupted!"

"Come along," he said with a wave of his hand, and began striding towards the back of the mall, his army of zombies following close behind him. The entire area behind the mall was abandoned and trash lined the decaying parking lot and sidewalks. There were no cars or people in sight and the woods behind the mall provided perfect cover. The doctor headed for the large store at the end of the mall. At one time it had been a Sears, but was now just an empty, closed up shell.

When the marching horde arrived at the nearest boarded up door, the doctor pointed at it, "Open that for me," he instructed his nearest zombie minion.

The zombie set down the dead body it was carrying and grabbed the edge of the wood nailed to the door. The zombie pulled and eventually the wood splintered and tore free from the door frame. The zombie lost several fingernails in the process but didn't even notice. The zombie then smashed the glass inside the door with its fists, creating an entrance for the doctor. Blood dripped from deep cuts on the zombies hand but the zombie didn't notice and the doctor didn't care.

The Plague Doctor walked into the murky, unlit store, broken glass crunching under his boots. His zombie creations, still carrying the dead bodies, followed behind him.

Chapter 7

The three urban explorers continued their journey down the abandoned lower level of the Linwood Mall. In the center of the thoroughfare was a rectangular advertising display with a photo of a couple in classic 90s clothing. Someone had drawn all over the picture with markers. Next to the sign was a shopping cart full of papers. Eddie went to investigate and after rifling through the heap, he determined the papers to be old billing and accounting files.
"I'm surprised no one has set that on fire," he said.
"Sounds like you want to," said Kayla with a smirk.
"I do," said Eddie with an evil grin, "but I don't have anything to start a fire with."
Kayla shook her head and laughed, "One of these days we'll have to find something you can set on fire for one of our videos."
"That would make an awesome photo though," Cole added, as he filmed the cart full of papers, "a burning shopping cart in the middle of an abandoned, derelict mall."
Kayla walked into one of the stores on their left. The walls had large mirrors on them, most of which were broken and cracked. There were four light red columns spaced evenly apart in the store.
"What do you think this store was?" she asked her friends.
"Maybe a clothing store."
"Or jewelry store. It's hard to say with everything stripped out."
"Yeah, it's hard to tell what a lot of these stores used to be."
As the trio was leaving the store, Eddie noticed a large pile of papers and cardboard boxes on the mall floor up ahead and went to check it out. He tentatively kicked the pile with his shoe.
"You sure like digging through the trash," said Kayla. "Maybe we should start a YouTube channel where we film you dumpster diving and all the things you find."

Eddie snorted, "Probably be a big hit too."

He kicked through the pile some more and then bent over and picked something up.

"These are film negatives," he said with surprise as he held them up in the air in front of the skylights. "Looks like random people. Weird."

Cole went over to take a look, "Back in the day malls had photo studios, where you could get your portraits taken."

"I've never seen one of those," Kayla said. "Before my time I guess."

"Oh yeah, they did *Glamour Shots*. Made you look like an 80s rock star; big hair, loud makeup, the whole thing," said Cole with a smile. "My sister had a couple of those back in high school. Google it, it's hilarious."

"When I was little we went to Sears one time for a family photo but that was a long time ago," remarked Kayla.

"How fitting," said Eddie, dropping the film negative back onto the pile of papers, "Sears is closed up and forgotten and so is this mall."

. . .

"Dude!" said Eddie, barely containing his excitement as he hopped up and down on his feet, gesturing wildly at the store in front of them. "*Dude!*"

"No way..." said Cole in awe.

Kayla looked at the store in front of them. The outer wall was covered in two shades of brown square tiles and the metal security gate was down; although it was pretty bent up like someone had tried to break through it. Interestingly the glass display windows were not busted but there were a few cracks in them and what appeared to be a bullet hole. Above the entrance was the faded image of where the store sign used to hang.

It said Kay Bee toys.

"Cool," she said casually, shrugging her shoulders, "a Kay Bee toy store."

Cole looked at her like she was some horrible swamp beast and shook his head in disappointment. "Uh...This is not just *some* toy store, this is an *iconic* toy store of the eighties. These disappeared a long time ago. Man, I *loved* this store!"

Eddie was grinning from ear to ear as he took photo after photo of the store front. "I never thought I'd see one of these again! I bought a lot of

Star Wars toys at Kay Bee."

"I loved their clearance section. That's where I spent most of my allowance," Cole said with a grin. "Those were great times."

"You guys really like this store, huh?" Kayla asked as she filmed the two going crazy over the empty toy store. "I've never seen one of these before."

"This right here makes the whole trip worth it," said Eddie, taking pictures from every possible angle.

Kayla stood back, smiling as her two friends enjoyed the discovery of their favorite childhood toy store.

A loud **CRASH** came from further down the mall.

Kayla turned towards the noise, "Did you guys hear that?" she said with apprehension.

Eddie stopped taking pics for a moment, "There someone else in the mall?"

"Could be…" said Kayla.

"Or rats," said Cole, "or wild dogs, or squatters, homeless people, escaped criminals, mutants…"

"This place is falling apart around us, maybe some ceiling tiles fell down." The three stood still for a few minutes, waiting to see if they heard the sound again. It was quiet save for a dripping sound coming from somewhere up ahead and to the right.

There were no further sounds so the three went back to filming and taking photos of the Kay Bee toy store.

"It'll be hard to top this," said Cole when he finished filming the toy store.

"For sure," said Eddie smiling. "This is turning out to be one unforgettable day. Let's go see what other cool stuff this mall has to offer!"

Chapter 8

The interior of the old Sears was dark and musty smelling. As the Plague Doctor made his way through the empty store his footsteps echoed in the empty, cavernous space and his feet kicked up dust which floated slowly through the air. His small army of zombies kicked up their own dust as they followed him, the dust filling the air behind them like a low lying brown fog. His zombies trailed obediently behind him, each still carrying a body that would soon become another zombie to join their ranks.

The doctor continued to explore the store, going around large square columns and two wooden display racks that had been left behind. A set of dismantled escalators that led to an upper floor caught the Plague Doctor's eye and he stopped to examine them.

He saw light at the far end of the store and walked in that direction. The abandoned Sears store had an entrance that led to the interior of the mall. All the glass doors were busted out and the light was coming from there. As the doctor got closer to this mall entrance, the light got much brighter and lit up a huge section of the store.

Dust covered the entire floor and there was a pile of broken shelves along one wall. A lot of ceiling tiles were missing and exposed wires hung down throughout the empty store.

The Plague Doctor walked around a section of the floor, somewhat lit by the light coming from inside the mall but also still shrouded in shadows.

"This will do nicely," he said, crossing back and forth over the space.

The doctor moved a few boxes and a metal rack out of the way, clearing a large area of the floor. He inspected the area one more time and nodded his head in approval.

The Plague Doctor motioned to the cleared space around him, "Set the patients down here in rows," he instructed his zombies. "Do be gentle."

The doctor got out his medical bag, "It is time to continue my work," he said as he removed a scalpel from inside the bag.

Chapter 9

"Hey, look up there!' Kayla said, pointing down the mall ahead of the three explorers. "It's the mall center."
Directly in front of the trio, about 50 feet away, the mall opened up into a large courtyard, well lit by a huge circular skylight in the roof high above.
"Ah...the hub," said Cole as he reached the courtyard and walked under the skylight, holding his arms out and turning in a circle under the light.
There were two escalators leading to the upper level but they had been shut down long ago.
The trio examined the escalators and shot some video and pictures of the dormant machines.
"I loved going on these things when I was a kid," said Kayla, smiling.
Eddie walked over to a large rectangle recessed into the mall floor. It was covered in a variety of square blue tiles. "Check it out, it's a fountain."
"Nice!" said Cole, joining Eddie and filming the empty, tile lined fountain. "You don't see these in malls anymore."
Kayla got inside the fountain and walked around. "When I was a little kid I always wanted to walk around the fountain in the mall we had in our town. I always thought that would be so fun."
"Haha," laughed Cole, "I wanted to do the same thing!"
Cole climbed into the fountain and walked around inside with Kayla.
"Any pennies in there?" Eddie asked the pair as they shuffled around inside.
"No," Kayla said, examining the floor of the empty fountain. "No pennies; just a dead bird and some empty bottles."
Kayla and Cole got out of the fountain and rejoined Eddie to explore more of the mall hub. There were several large empty and cracked planters by one corner of the empty fountain, all broken and laying in a messy pile.
A few metal benches lay scattered around, one had a broken leg and was laying on it's side.
"I bet this is where everyone hung out," said Cole, panning around and

filming the large space. "This space probably used to be full of benches and places to sit."

"Dude!" shouted Eddie, pointing excitedly off to the side. "It's the food court!"

Over on the side of the open courtyard area was the food court. Tucked underneath the second floor, it looked like a huge cave. There were seven empty restaurant stalls and in front of those several old tables and a few decaying chairs still remained.

The three went over to the empty food court, laughing and joking as Cole turned in a slow half-circle, capturing the entire food court on video.

"Look!" said Kayla as she walked over to one of the eateries. "You can see the outline of where a Taco Bell sign used to be."

"Check out those brown tiles!' said Eddie. Behind the counter, the sides and back walls of the old Taco Bell were covered in large brown tiles.

Kayla crawled over the counter and looked around inside the restaurant. There was nothing left except a few greasy stains on the floor and a beat up stainless steel prep table. She took out her phone and snapped a few pics, "I used to love Taco Bell," Kayla said. "We used to eat burritos there all the time when I was in High School."

"Yo quiero Taco Bell," said Cole, laughing.

Eddie walked over to the other food establishments, shining his flashlight inside each one. Cole was following behind him, filming the entire food court and making sure to capture the old food signs and retro decor that each restaurant had. There was an Italian place, decked out in red, white and green tiles and a Chinese eatery in mostly red tiles with a few white tiles for trim. Cole was about to film a Mexican restaurant when Eddie screamed up in front of him.

"***Aarghh!***"

Cole ran up behind Eddie, "What is it?" he asked worriedly, looking around the food court.

"I saw something in the Pizza place!" said Eddie, pointing nervously to the eatery he had been taking photos of. "Something was moving in the kitchen."

Kayla rushed over, "You sure?"

"It was a huge shadow, it looked like a person."

"Could be a homeless person or a squatter," said Kayla, staring intently at the Pizza joint.

Cole walked up to the counter of the pizza joint. He took his flashlight out and shone the light inside the kitchen.

"You sure you want to do that?" asked Eddie, standing ten feet away and not taking one step closer.

"I don't see anything," Cole said.

He then climbed over the counter.

"I wouldn't do that either…" said Eddie nervously.

Cole walked slowly and deliberately into the kitchen, his flashlight illuminating the small space.

"There's nothing in here," he said. "Just a bunch of trash and rat droppings."

Cole climbed back over the counter.

Eddie was shaking his head, "I know I saw something."

"Well, whatever it was, it's gone."

The three continued filming the rest of the food court; but the whole time Eddie kept glancing back at the pizza place, expecting something or someone to jump out and come after them.

Kayla had been eyeing the escalators as they returned to the central hub. "Hey, let's check upstairs out," she said, looking up the escalators to the second floor balcony. "I've been dying to go up those since I first saw them."

"Allright," said Cole, "we can finish the downstairs later."

Eddie glanced over at Kayla, "Race you!" he shouted and then took off running towards the escalator. Kayla ran after him, running up the left escalator while Eddie ran up the right one. When Eddie reached the top of the escalator he jumped up and down, yelling, "I win! I'm the king of the mall!"

Kayla was only a few seconds behind him and she punched him on the shoulder when she reached him. "Cheater!" she said, while he shrugged and grinned. They both stood at the edge of the escalators, catching their breath while they looked down at Cole walking up the escalators to join them.

Chapter 10

The Plague Doctor smiled as he admired his creations.

Before him stood 27 zombies awaiting his command. There would have been 28 but one of his operations had been unsuccessful. It had been a long time since the doctor'd had this many creations under his control and he was quite thrilled about it.

The doctor rubbed his hands together with joy, "Now, what shall we do first?" he said quietly to himself. He'd been hard at work for most of the day and could definitely use a break.

The Plague Doctor looked across the empty store towards the entrance that led out to the inside of the abandoned mall.

"Perhaps we should see what else is in this establishment. We should be able to find something to amuse ourselves with for a while. Then afterwards I will need to find more subjects for my work."

The doctor motioned to his zombies with his hand, "This way my friends," he said, pointing towards the mall, "let us take a stroll through this forgotten mecca of commerce and see what awaits us out there."

The Plague Doctor started to cross the empty store, walking towards the entrance to the abandoned Linwood Mall, his large entourage of zombies following behind him.

Chapter 11

"**Aarghh!**" screamed Cole.

As he raced up to the top of the escalators he was pointing behind his two friends and waving his hands animatedly.

Kayla and Eddie had been standing at the top, joking with each other as they waited for him.

"What?!" said Eddie in alarm, as he and Kayla quickly spun around to look behind them, expecting something terrible.

"Whoa..." said Kayla, when she saw what Cole had been yelling about.

At the top of the escalators was a large store. And someone had taken a mannequin and hung it from the ceiling inside the store.

"Nice," said Eddie, shaking his head in disapproval.

"Yeah, that's not creepy at all," added Kayla. "I didn't even see that when I ran up here."

"Me neither."

"Sorry," said Cole, joining the other two standing in front of the store, staring at the mannequin. "I saw that coming up the escalator behind you guys and it freaked me out."

"This mall *is* pretty creepy," said Eddie as he tentatively stepped through one of the broken store windows and walked up to the hanging mannequin. It was just the upper torso and head, and someone had written the word FAKER across the front with a purple sharpie marker. "I'd hate to be locked in here at night."

"I don't know," said Kayla with a sly grin, "other than the weird noises, mold, giant rats, possible squatters and glass everywhere, it could be cool to spend the night in here."

"Go for it," said Eddie, walking back to join his two friends, "I'll be at home in my bed. *Safe* in my bed."

"Ah, come on Eddie," said Kayla. "It could be fun!"

"Yeah," Cole added, "an abandoned mall sleepover would be an *awesome* video! That would pull in a lot of subscribers!"

"No thanks," said Eddie, rolling his eyes as he walked away from the store. "That sounds like the opposite of awesome. I don't mind exploring during the day, but I don't do creepy night time stuff. *No way.*"

The three began walking down the upper level, passing an old beauty salon that still had a few mirrors and sinks covering half of one wall.

"Besides," Eddie continued, "this mall might be haunted."

Kayla let out a snort, "Haunted? I've never heard of a haunted mall."

Eddie waved his hands around, there was trash littering the floor and busted glass everywhere. Some of the walls on the second floor were moldy and there were even a few spots where weeds were growing out of cracks in the floor tiles. The graffiti was much worse on the second level. To add to the mess were several large puddles of water on the floor and a lot of the hand rails along the edge of the balcony were missing, making it very dangerous.

"Look at this place, you know someone has to have died in here at some point…"

Kayla shook her head, "I never read or heard anything about anyone dying in here."

"Well, let's hope we're not the first," Cole muttered as he continued to film everything as they walked on.

. . .

"Look at this!" said Kayla, pointing energetically at a store front. Eddie and Cole hurried over to see what she was so excited about.

"Oh….Wow!" said Eddie in a hushed tone, before starting to snap pics with his phone.

"Now that is some freaky stuff," Cole said with a huge smile. "This is going to be so great for the video. This is going to be our biggest video yet!"

The store in front of them used to be a large clothing store.

Although the store no longer had any clothes inside, it wasn't *completely* empty.

The front half of the store was full of mannequins.

Six rows of mannequins; all wearing different clothes, all standing, and all were staring straight out at the mall.

Eddie turned and grinned at Kayla, "Still want to spend the night in here?" Then in a lower, creepier voice he added, "Imagine finding *this* in the middle of the night. The cult of the possessed mannequins."

Kayla chuckled, "That *would* be pretty creepy. It'd be even creepier if they were all wearing the exact same thing...like brown robes or something. Now *that* would be *freaky!*"

She went into the store and walked between the rows of lifeless clothing models, taking more pics with her phone. Cole and Eddie joined her and they inspected the eerie display of unmoving figures.

"This is so weird," said Eddie in a whisper.

"We should move them," suggested Kayla. "Put them all in a circle."

"*Yes!*" Cole agreed. "Have them all facing the center and we can put one mannequin in the middle."

"Sure, why not? Let's make this mall even more disturbing," said Eddie, shaking his head.

Kayla ignored Eddie's comment and continued, "Yeah, this will be perfect, we can freak out whoever comes in the mall next. Get *them* wondering *who* did it and *why*."

"Maybe we'll see it on someone else's YouTube video," said Cole as he grabbed the nearest mannequin and moved it to the side of the room.

"We'll have to clear some space first," he said.

Kayla picked up a mannequin and moved it to the side of the room as well.

Eddie reluctantly joined the other two.

"This is going to be so epic!" said Kayla joyfully as she picked up another mannequin.

The three went about the work of moving the mannequins out of the center of the store. Once they had cleared enough space, they started back at the middle and began forming a circle with the mannequins.

Eddie selected a mannequin that was wearing a hot pink tank top and neon yellow leggings to be the one standing in the middle of the circle.

CRASH

"*Aarghh!*" screamed Eddie in surprise, knocking over a mannequin with a loud crash.

Kayla jumped back and slammed into a mannequin as well, sending it smashing into another mannequin and they both toppled to the floor, landing with a loud bang that echoed throughout the store.

"Dang it guys!" said Cole angrily. "Calm down! You're freaking me out with all your jumping around every time you hear a noise."

Cole was staring at the two with a deep frown.

"Sorry," said Eddie sheepishly, "the noise startled me."

"Me too," said Kayla, looking sideways at Eddie, "but Eddie's scream startled me more."

"It sounded like it came from down by the end of the mall," said Eddie quietly.

"That was the same sound we heard earlier by the Kay Bee toy store," Kayla whispered. "It was loud, too loud to be a rat or a dog."

"There must be someone else in here," said Cole. "Could be kids causing trouble or someone living here."

"Or security," said Kayla with a worried expression on her face.

The three stood still, surrounded by the unmoving, unblinking faces of the mannequins. After several quiet minutes they hadn't heard another sound.

"OK," said Cole, "let's finish with the mannequins and move on, but keep your eyes open."

Chapter 12

"That's perfect!" Kayla smiled and nodded her head in approval as she stood outside the clothing store, admiring the circle of mannequins inside.
"Wish I could be here when the next person finds this," said Cole smiling wistfully, standing beside Kayla and Eddie.
"I have to admit," Eddie said, squinting in a half smile, half grimace, "it does look pretty dang creepy."
The three friends laughed and joked for a minute before moving on down the mall. They passed a few empty stores, one of which was a small jewelry store that had all of it's glass displays smashed.
"Hey guys!" Eddie exclaimed, pointing across the mall, to the other side of the upper level.
"Look over there! It's an old Gadzooks!"
"*No way!*" said Kayla, almost drooling. "That was one of my favorite stores *ever!*"
Cole spun around and looked at her in surprise, "You liked Gadzooks?"
"Heck yeah! Who doesn't like Gadzooks?!" Kayla said with pure joy. She started to walk down the mall concourse towards the elevated walkway that would cross from the side of the mall they were on to the other side where the Gadzooks was.
Kayla wanted to run over to the Gadzooks store but had to take her time, not only were handrails missing from the edge of the balcony, but there were also quite a few large puddles of water on the floor. She certainly didn't want to slip and slide over the edge of the balcony.
Kaya eventually made her way to the other side and stood in front of her favorite, long forgotten clothing store. Cole and Eddie followed her and joined her in front of the Gadzooks.
"Gadzooks is where I bought most of my clothes for junior high. This store had the coolest stuff," Kayla remarked.

She stepped back and took photos of the store font, with it's shiny black tiles.

"Wow, most of the neon sign is still intact," she said in wonder, snapping pics of what was left of the red neon Gadzooks sign.

Eddie was peering through the glass and into the vacant store.

"I've never even been in a Gadzooks," he said. Eddie kept looking inside the store and then in a quieter tone said, "My mom made me get all my clothes at K-Mart."

"Ouch," said Cole, walking up and joining Eddie at the front glass doors. He pushed on one of the doors and it moved.

"Come on," he said, turning to Eddie, "now you can finally say you've been in a Gadzooks." Cole pushed the door open and walked into the empty store. He held the door open for Eddie and Kayla.

"Yeah! Come on!" said Kayla, grabbing Eddie by the arm and pulling him into the store.

The three friends walked around the vacant store.

"Not quite how I remember it," Kayla kidded. She strolled around the store, gazing dreamily at the empty walls, "I did buy a Red Hot Chilli Peppers shirt here once. Such a cool shirt too. I wore that thing everywhere."

Eddie was in the back of the store, inspecting what appeared to be a stack of orange traffic cones.

CRASH

"What the-?!" Eddie yelled, as he stumbled forward and knocked over the cones. "It's that noise again!"

"That was louder than before," said Kayla, looking around nervously. "*It's either getting closer to us, or we're getting closer to it.*"

"It sounded like it was downstairs," Cole said, walking back towards the entrance to the store. "Let's check it out."

"What?" hissed Eddie. "Are you crazy?! It could be a serial killer!"

"It might be security, and I *don't* want to go to jail," said Kayla. "*Again.*"

She waited a moment and then let out a sign when no one laughed at her joke.

Cole was already at the door and was cautiously poking his head outside and peering to the left and right.

"Nothing," he whispered.

"Good, now get back in here!" hissed Eddie.

Cole ignored him and stepped out of the store, being extra careful not to step on any glass or trash that might make a noise. He stood in the middle of the walkway, looking back and forth in both directions and also across the mall at the other side. Cole was straining, listening hard for any sound.

Kayla and Eddie both quietly exited the Gadzooks and joined him outside the store.

CRASH

Eddie jumped in surprise, startling Kayla who jerked back in shock.

"Stop doing that!" she growled, slapping him on the arm.

Cole slowly inched towards the edge of the second story balcony. He made sure to avoid any puddles of water. Without any guardrails, he wanted to stay as far back from the edge as possible and surely didn't want to slip in any water. As he got closer to the edge he leaned his head forward, trying to peer downstairs. He still couldn't see anything so he took another step closer to the edge and peered over.

It was then that Cole finally managed to get a look at what was making the noise they kept hearing.

"What the…?" he stuttered.

Chapter 13

That can't be right, Cole thought as he stood as close to the edge of the balcony as he dared.

He could only see them by stretching out as far as he possibly could.

He took a step backwards, so he couldn't see them and they couldn't see him.

He blinked several times.

Kayla and Eddie quietly walked up beside him.

"What is it?" Kayla whispered anxiously. "*What'd you see?*"

"Was it an axe murderer?" asked Eddie, nervously.

"Uh...not quite."

Kayla took a step and leaned forward so she could see for herself what was down below.

"What-? *No way!*" she whispered as she stepped back to stand beside Cole.

She and Cole looked at each other, neither one saying a word.

Eddie looked at them expectantly, "Well?" he asked impatiently. "*What is it?!*"

"Uh...zombies?"

"Yeah, zombies."

Eddie stared at the two, a blank expression on his face. After a second he stepped forward and took a look at the lower level.

He then stepped back to stand beside his friends.

No one said anything.

Eddie took another step forward and glanced over the edge again.

He rejoined his friends. Eddie looked at Kayla and then he looked at Cole.

"Zombies," said Cole quietly.

Down below, on the lower level, there was a large crowd of young people slowly walking through the mall. They walked in a jerky, unstable kind of way with their mouths half open. There were fresh stitches on their faces and arms and they made a soft gurgling sound as shuffled along. They were moving slowly and stepping on debris and trash and bumping into things, making loud noises when they did.

After a few silent moments Eddie finally asked, "Are they filming a video or something?"

Cole shrugged, "Maybe…"

"Well what else could they be doing?"

"No idea…"

Kayla took another peek, "They're all following behind that one guy in front, the one dressed in black."

"What is that guy supposed to be?" asked Eddie, peering over the side. "Some sort of steampunk cosplay?"

"Looks like he's wearing a masquerade mask," said Kayla.

"This is so weird," muttered Eddie, shaking his head.

Cole had been silently thinking but then suddenly spoke up, "I know what he is! He's a plague doctor."

"A what?!" asked Eddie.

"A plague doctor," answered Cole. "Back during the time of the Black Plague, doctors would try and treat people or carry the dead bodies away. They wore those masks. They thought the plague was transmitted through smell so they had those long noses on their mask stuffed with herbs and stuff so they couldn't smell anything."

Eddie just stared at Cole.

"That's a plague doctor down there?" Eddie asked, incredulously.

"Looks like it," Cole answered tentatively.

"So you're saying that is a time traveling plague doctor?" said Kayla with a laugh. "Maybe *we* traveled in time. Maybe this *mall* is a time machine."

Eddie looked stunned, "We traveled in time?"

Cole slapped Eddie on the arm, "No dummy! It's obviously a guy in a costume."

Eddie shook his head, "Sometimes I wonder why I'm friends with you guys."

"Because you love us," said Kayla with a huge grin.

"Should we say something?" asked Eddie.

"I don't know. I guess, or we could just continue on, ignore them," suggested

Cole.

"Ignore them? There's like 50 people down there!" said Eddie worriedly. "They might come after us!"

"They don't own the mall," Cole said sternly.

"Did you hear the part about *50* of them?" said Eddie agitatedly.

Cole leaned out again, this time holding his camera out so he could film the large group below them. Kayla joined him and took some video with her phone.

"This is pretty wild," she whispered.

"No kidding," Cole said, "our video is going to be huge! Zombies at the abandoned mall, our views will be through the roof! Here comes the ad revenue!"

Eddie leaned out on Cole's other side and the three watched as the group of zombies trailed behind the plague doctor, who appeared to be the leader.

"That many people are sure to attract security or the police," said Eddie.

"There may not be security at this mall," said Cole.

"I don't see any cameras," said Kayla anxiousy, "or anyone else down there filming."

"Maybe they're rehearsing," suggested Eddie, hopeful but nervous.

"Maybe…"

"I think we should say hello," said Kayla. Something about how realistic the zombies were was making her very apprehensive.

"Yeah, maybe we can be in their video," Eddie said, smiling tensely, trying to hide his rising fear.

As the three mall explorers continued to watch, the masked figure said something to the zombies and the mob suddenly broke up into groups of two and three and spread out and began going into all the stores.

"What are they doing?"

"Are they looking for something?" asked Eddie. "Or someone? I don't like this…"

Kayla tried to lighten the mood, "Maybe they're looking for that Christmas tree."

The other two didn't laugh.

"It doesn't look like they're rehearsing," said Eddie anxiously. "Maybe we should just get out of here and come back tomorrow."

"Hang on," said Cole, still filming the scene below, "let's watch them for a little bit. I want to see what they're up to."

The zombie horde was slowly making its way down the mall, from the end, towards the central courtyard. The figure with the plague doctor mask and the black coat kept walking forward while the zombies continued to go in and out of each store, obviously looking for something but always coming out of the stores empty handed.

"Hey," whispered Eddie, "how are we going to get out of here with all of them down there?"

"Don't know," said Cole, still intently watching the activity below.

"Guys, this is getting pretty freaky," Eddie said. "What if it's some crazy cult?"

Cole turned to Eddie, "Dude! Relax!" he said. "Let's just watch them and see what's up. Then we can freak out."

"I think it's time to freak out now," said Kayla, pointing down towards the large crowd below.

"Oh no," whispered Eddie frightfully as he turned back to look at the group downstairs.

. . .

All the zombies had stopped and were standing still.

And they were *all* looking up at Kayla, Eddie and Cole.

All of them.

Their masked leader was staring at them as well, his head cocked to the side, studying them.

"Uh…," stammered Eddie. "What do we do?"

Cole waved slowly and hesitantly at the group below, "Hello?"

There was no response.

Kayla leaned forward, "Hi! We're just making a Youtube video about the mall, we won't be in your way."

No response.

Cole glanced at his two friends, "The zombies look really mad. Like, *really* mad," he whispered.

"Did we mess up their movie somehow?" Eddie asked nervously.

"No way," said Kayla. "Maybe they're just messing with us."

Cole leaned forward, waving at the zombies and the masked

figure, "Sorry if we messed up your movie or whatever you're doing. We're leaving now."

No response.

"So what now?" asked Kayla, eyeing the strange group below with growing dread.

"Let's just move on, we'll go down towards the end of the mall, leave these weirdos alone," Eddie said, as he started to walk away, "Those guys are giving me the creeps, big time."

Cole was busy looking around, "Over there," he said pointing to a group of large empty planters by the edge of the upper walkway. "Let's walk away and double back and hide behind those planters. Then we can see what they do when they think we've left."

Eddie let out a groan as Cole waved to the mob below, turned and began to walk away, slowly getting further away from the balcony edge until he was out of sight. Then Cole ran over to the front of the nearest store but stayed by the store, out of sight. Then he crawled over to the planters and ducked behind them. Eddie and Kayla followed his lead, and copied Cole until all three were huddling behind the large blue planters.

"Now we wait a bit and then see what they do," Cole said, seriously.

Chapter 14

"Oohhh!" said the Plague Doctor, with pleasant surprise, as he looked up at the second floor of the mall. He watched as Kayla and her two friends tried to hide behind some large concrete pots that used to contain plants and flowers. "I spy three little mice snooping around where they don't belong. I knew we would find something to amuse us in here."

Without taking his eyes off of the three humans upstairs, the doctor pointed to the upper level, towards the hiding trio. He addressed his waiting zombie horde, "My friends, we have a new game to play! We must apprehend those three with all due haste. We cannot let them leave this place and report our activities to the authorities."

The doctor frowned and his tone of voice changed to an angry, ominous tone, "I'm not ready to return to the facility. *Not just yet.*"
The Plague Doctor finished speaking and turned to look away from the three upstairs and faced his creations, "Now go *get* them," he said intensely. "Bring them to me."

. . .

"**Aaargh!** He's pointing at us!" said Cole, ducking back behind the large blue planter he was hiding behind.
"*Oh man*," said Eddie, worriedly, "who *is* that guy? What do they want?!"
The zombies started to walk towards the central courtyard where the escalators were.

One of the zombies tripped on a section of broken glass and crashed to the floor. When he got up, blood was running down it's legs and arms. The zombie didn't notice or care about the cuts or blood and just continued walking.
"That's not normal," said Eddie, panic rising in his voice. "Did you see that? That guy's bleeding all over the place and no one's doing anything."

Cole and Kayla were watching in silence.

"I'm freaking out guys. These might be real zombies!" said Eddie, rocking back and forth on his feet nervously. "Those *can't* be real zombies, *right?!*"

"I don't know, they look like real zombies, not some cheap makeup effects," said Cole. "And that guy is bleeding and they're all still ignoring it."

"No way..*right?* Are you kidding?" asked Eddie, his voice going high with fright. *"Zombies?"*

"Gotta kill the brain…" said Kayla helpfully. "It's the only way to stop them."

"Everyone knows that," said Cole.

"Wait, are we *ok* with the fact that there are real zombies down there?" asked Eddie, starting to freak out. "Are we *really* talking about killing zombies right now?"

'I don't know," said Cole, grabbing Eddie by the shoulder, "but they look real and I don't want to get myself *or* you guys hurt or killed. So for now, I'm acting like they're real zombies."

"This can't be happening," said Eddie disbelivigningly.

"So what's our play?" asked Kayla.

"Call the cops- *duh!*" said Eddie, throwing his arms in the air. "What other play is there?"

Kayla nodded her head, took her phone out and dialed 911.

"Yes, we're trapped inside Linwood Mall. Yes. No, we're fine but there is a large group of..of scary people in here. We can't get out."

Cole and Eddie leaned in, trying to hear the operator as Kayla continued.

"Uh, I don't know, maybe 20 or 30 people. I can't see any weapons but they look angry and dangerous and they're coming after us."

Kayla was silent for a moment, "OK, thanks." then she hung up.

"Well?!" asked Eddie.

"I don't know if she believed me but she said a patrol car was in route. They'd be here soon."

"Soon? What does that mean? Five minutes or one hour?" asked Eddie with frustration.

"I have no clue, she only said soon."

"So what now?" Eddie asked.

Cole leaned over and spied on the horde below. "They're getting real close to the escalators. I think they might be coming up here."

"Do we wait for the cops or run for it?" Eddie asked, agitated, glancing down the mall toward the escalators.

"What if it takes the cops an hour to get here?" asked Cole. "That's plenty of time to get killed by a zombie mob."

"Then I guess we run. We should get out of here, *as far away as possible*" said Eddie, as he looked expectantly from Kayla to Cole, his eyes wide with fright. "You guys just heard the part about the death by zombies, right? We have to get out of here *now!*"

"But how?' asked Kayla. "We came in on the ground floor. And that's where the zombies are."

"Then maybe we could hide somewhere?" suggested Eddie.

"No, no way I'm hiding," Cole said, "we hole up somewhere and they trap us, it's *game over man*. We're *dead*."

"What about the roof?" asked Eddie. "We could get up on the roof and barricade the door, wait until someone finds us or maybe find a way to climb down and run away."

"There might be more than one entrance to the roof though, we could get trapped up there with them..." said Kayla thoughtfully. "And where exactly is the roof access anyway?"

"We could fight them…" said Cole quietly. "We've all seen enough zombie movies and played plenty of video games, we know what to do."

"We have no *weapons*," Eddie said, frustrated. "Pepper spray and a taser wont do squat against a zombie army." Eddie ran his fingers through his hair, "And video games are totally different than real life. I can't believe we're talking about *zombies*."

"We need guns and swords," said Kayla.

"Well, we won't find those anywhere in here," Eddie snapped, clearly starting to panic.

"Ok, then we run," said Cole. "Obviously we can't go back down the escalators at the central mall courtyard. Is there another way to get to the lower level?"

"Oh yeah! The anchor stores like Sears and Penneys usually have their own escalators," said Kayla.

"I forgot about that," said Eddie, relieved. "Let's get to one of those, get downstairs and bust out a door or window and get the heck out of here."

"Sounds like a plan," said Cole, "which store?"

"We're in the middle of the mall, there should be at least one anchor store in both directions," said Kayla, "pick a side and let's go!"

"Ok, let's keep going the way we were headed, so we won't have to pass back by the courtyard. And we might as well see some of the mall while we make our escape. Be good for the video."

"The video? *Seriously?*" said Eddie in disbelief. "You're still worried about our *video?!*"

Cole shrugged his shoulders, "We're here, might as well keep filming." Then he added without missing a beat. "This will be the best Youtube video ever!"

"If we live to upload it!" Eddie hissed. "We've got a bigger issue to deal besides our video!"

"Relax, we just have to make it until the cops show up. Worst case someone else finds the video and then they'll know what happened in here."

"*Worse case?!* What *is* going to happen in here?" asked Eddie frantically.

"Nothing Eddie," Kayla said brusquely, "nothing's going to happen. You guys ready or what?"

Cole was peeking around the planters again, "Sure, let me see what they're up to real quick."

He slowly glanced around the planter, "They're coming!" he said under his breath, "Go!"

Cole pushed his two friends, "Come on, they're at the escalators, but they still have to get upstairs, we have a good head start."

The three friends scooted back over to the front of the nearest store.

"Hey guys?" Eddie said hesitatingly.

"What?" whispered Cole impatiently.

"I just want you to know that I love you guys."

"Are you for real right now?" asked Kayla, somewhat angrily. "We don't have time for this!"

Cole was surprised by his words too, "What?"

"You know...in case we don't make it," Eddie explained sheepishly, staring at the floor.

Kayla shook her head, "Come on, let's go," she said as she stood up.

Cole patted Eddie on the back as they got up, "I love you too bro."

The three stayed as close to the front of the stores as they could, trying their best to stay clear of the balcony and out of site from the zombies below. Cole kept his camera on and tried to hold it as steady as possible. They ran past an old Camelot Music store that used to sell cassettes and then later CDs.

"Ah man, I remember that store!" Cole said with a smile.

"Who cares right now!" said Eddie, barely even looking at the store. He was focused on the path in front of them and nothing else.

"Maybe we can come back when this is all over," said Kayla.

"Doubt it," said Cole, "the cops will lock this place down super tight after this. Our video might end up being the last footage of Linwood Mall ever."

"Famous!" whispered Cole with delight.

Chapter 15

"Why are they coming after us? We didn't do anything!" shouted Eddie as he ran behind Cole and Kayla.

"I don't know! Why don't you stop and ask them?" said Cole curtly, as he led the three down the mall, jumping over a pile of boxes and slowing down to skirt around two large algae covered pools of water. The trio passed two more stores but had to stop in front of the third one.

The entire mall walkway, from the inside of the store all the way to the edge of the balcony was covered in water. The water was slowly dripping over the edge of the balcony, forming a tiny waterfall. The sound of the water splashing on the lower level echoed up through the mall.

"Whoa," said Kayla as they stopped in front of the large mass of water.

She shrugged her shoulders and stepped into the water. Slowly, she sidestepped through the cold water, trying to go slow and not slip or make big splashes. Cole and Eddie followed her lead.

"Oh man, my shoes!" Eddie whined.

As they passed the storefront Cole glanced inside, the entire store was full of water.

"Must have had a water pipe break. What a mess."

Eddie paused and looked behind them. Far down the mall he could just barely see the escalators at the central courtyard. Tiny shapes were moving up the escalators.

"They're almost up the escalators!" he hissed, turning back around and shuffling his feet faster through the water, splashing water everywhere as he hurried to get through.

Once past the massive puddle, the three tried to run but their shoes were too slippery so they had to walk. Their shoes squeaked loudly as they hustled along the concourse. Any other time and the situation would have been hilarious, but no one was laughing now. They walked as fast as they could until their shoes were dry enough to run again.

They ran on until they reached the store at the very end of the mall.
It was a Sears store.
"No, no, no...," Eddie said quietly, shaking his head sadly as they approached the store.
"Oh crap." Cole exclaimed with dismay.
And finally Kayla added, "This isn't good."

. . .

The three friends stood in front of the Sears store.
The entrance was completely boarded up.
The three tried to pull on the plywood nailed to the walls but they were secured too well and there was no way to get a good hold on the boards.
Eddie looked behind them, "I see movement!" he said alarmed. "What do we do now?"
"We can't stand here waiting for the cops to show up," Cole said, looking down the mall at the advancing zombies.
"Well we can't hide in any of these stores," said Kayla, gesturing to the empty stores around them. "They've already seen us come down here, if they start searching the stores and find us we're in trouble."
"That's true," said Cole, "and we don't have any weapons to defend ourselves with."
"We have to go back, get to one of the other two-story department stores and get downstairs that way," said Kayla.
"*Go back?* That's where the zombies are!" said Eddie frantically pointing towards the escalators, far down the mall.
"We'll run down the opposite side of the mall, try and get past them," said Cole.
"That could work," Eddie thought for a second, "unless they get in front of us *and* behind us."
"They definitely *will* if we keep standing here, let's go already!" Kayla said, turning to the right side of the store and breaking into a run. She passed the Sears store and ran down the opposite side of the mall, with Cole and Eddie jogging behind her.

Up ahead, on the side of the mall they had just left, Kayla could see the zombies getting closer to them. The zombies were running but they weren't too fast and every now and then they would trip on their own feet and stumble.

"It looks like they're splitting up!" said Cole, pointing in front of the trio.

Further down the mall two zombies had started to cross over to the same side of the mall the three friends were on while another four zombies continued down the opposite side, trying to come up behind the trio.

"They're going to surround us!" Eddie shrieked. "*I told you!*"

"We can stay ahead of the four behind us but we're going to have to do something about the two that are crossing over in front of us," said Kayla. "We have to get past them."

The three friends sped past an old candle store that had a giant picture of a candle plastered on one wall. Inside the store were two large metal trash cans, beat up and bent.

"Wait!" shouted Cole. "I have an idea."

He stopped and ran back into the candle store. Cole grabbed one of the trash cans, "Follow my lead," he said to Kayla, as he exited the store, carrying the metal trash can.

Kayla ran into the candle store and picked up the other trash can. Then she followed Cole as he raced towards the two zombies approaching in front of them.

Cole spotted a place up ahead that had large puddles of water on the floor and stopped just before he got to them.

The zombies weren't very decayed and other than a few stitches and bruises on their faces and grey, vacant eyes, they looked like regular young people. The zombies growled and hissed at Cole as they approached, stepping in the puddles of water.

"Use the cans to knock them down," Cole shouted over his shoulder at Kayla.

When he was close to the zombie in front, Cole swung the metal can as hard as he could, hitting the zombie in the head and knocking it down. Kayla was right beside him and swinging her can as hard as she could, she smashed it into the other zombie. It let out a growl as it was knocked to the ground.

Cole hit his zombie again, then he put his can on the floor and used it to push the zombie along the wet floor. The zombie tried to get up but the floor was too wet and slippery and the zombie couldn't stand up fast enough.

The zombie flopped around on it's side and back. Cole kept pushing until he got the zombie to the edge of the rail less balcony and the zombie fell over the side, waving its arms wildy and kicking its legs in the air.

"Whoa," Kayla muttered.

She followed Cole's example and used her trash can to push the other zombie along the wet floor as well. The zombie growled at her and gnashed it's teeth. The zombie swiped it's hands at her but wasn't close enough to reach her. The zombie managed to get up on one knee but Kayla hit it again with the metal can, knocking it back to the floor. Then she put her can on the floor and pushed it against the zombie and kept pushing until the zombie went over the side.

Kayla and Cole dropped their trash cans and stood panting, looking over the side of the balcony at the two zombies laying on the floor below.

"Hopefully they broke a leg or two and won't be able to chase us anymore," said Cole.

Kayla slapped Cole on the shoulder, "Nice move!" she said excitedly. "We just took down two zombies!"

Cole nodded, "Surprised that worked."

Eddie had ran up behind the pair.

He stared at the two.

"Wow," he muttered, "that was intense."

"Two down," said Kayla with a grin. "*Literally*."

"What about the four coming up behind us?" asked Eddie nervously. "I'm going to need my own trash can."

"Well it's going to get worse than that Eddie," said Cole, pointing down the mall at the central courtyard. "There's a lot more zombies coming up the escalators."

Chapter 16

The Plague Doctor slowly walked down the mall, in the direction of the Sears store he and his zombies had originally come out of. He was keeping an eye on the three young people running along the upstairs walkway. He watched as two of his zombies crossed over to the opposite side of the mall to try and get in front of the three. Another four zombies were trying to come up behind the three people.

His zombies weren't the fastest or the smartest, but they were strong and completely obedient to him. They wouldn't stop chasing those three until the doctor ordered them to stop.

Interesting, the doctor thought, as he watched one of the young men and a woman come out of a store carrying large metal cans. The two used the cans to hit his zombies with and then unbelievingly used the same cans to push the zombies over the side of the balcony.

"Hahaha," the doctor laughed out loud, *Pretty smart, pretty smart indeed. This could turn out to be very interesting.*

The doctor watched as the two zombies fell over the side and landed on the lower floor with a sickening thud. One of the zombies slowly stood up but it had a broken leg and quickly fell back to the ground. Since it couldn't walk, it used its hands to pull itself along the floor and half crawled back towards the doctor.

The other zombie stood up. Broken bones protruded from it's left arm. The arm hung useless at the zombies' side. Unbothered by the broken arm, the zombie started to run slowly and awkwardly, its broken arm flapping against its hip. The zombie made its way back towards the escalator to rejoin the chase.

"Oh boy," said the doctor smiling with glee, "this is going to be so much fun!"

He then turned and pointed to another six zombies standing behind him, "Get up there and get those three."

The doctor smiled and turned back to watch the excitement unfolding upstairs.

Chapter 17

"*Oh no!* They're in front of us again!" Eddie shouted with alarm, pointing in front of the trio as they ran down the mall.

Up ahead, six more zombies had just left the courtyard escalators and were crossing over the mall in an attempt to get in front of the three friends.

Cole and Kayla had tried to take the trash cans with them but they were heavy and cumbersome so they'd decided to ditch them so they could move faster.

Kayla looked at the stores around them, looking for anything that might help them. There was an old Macy's on their left side, just in front of them. Her eyes lit up with excitement.

"Macy's!" She hollered, "Macy's will have an escalator! It's two stories!"

"Yes!" said Cole.

Eddie let out a huge sigh of relief.

The three rushed ahead and when they got to the old Macy's store they entered through a pair of doors that had been broken open.

"Thank goodness it's not boarded up!" exclaimed Eddie with relief, stepping on pieces of glass as he entered the store behind Cole.

There were piles of trash littering the floor and broken boards were everywhere. Wires hung from the ceiling and busted glass littered the tiled floor.

The light coming in from the mall only lit up a small portion of the front of the store so Kayla and the other two quickly got out their flashlights and turned them on.

Eddie took a glance behind them.

"Guys!" he screeched, "They're still coming, they're getting closer!"

"Come on!" shouted Kayla, breaking into a sprint as she dashed deeper into the store. "The escalators should be in the middle or close to the back of the store."

The three ran, using their flashlights to illuminate a path for them.

"I don't see anything!" Eddie cried with despair, as he shone his light all around them as they ran.

"It has to be here," Cole said, "unless this store isn't two stories."

"Oh great," moaned Eddie, "then we'll be trapped in here."

The three continued to run towards the back of the store.

Eddie heard something behind them and turned to look. The zombies had reached the doors and were entering the store.

"They're inside!" he screamed.

Kayla didn't even bother to look back, she just kept running and searching for the escalators that would take them downstairs.

They have to be here, she thought desperately. *They have to be!*

"I see something!" said Cole excitedly, running in front of his friends. Directly in front of him were four large square columns.

"Looks like the spot!" said Kayla with relief.

As Cole and the others reached the columns they came to a sudden stop.

"Come on!" said Cole with frustration.

"*Seriously?!*" Kayla said, shaking her fist angrily.

Where there used to be a pair of escalators; one going from the upper floor to the lower floor and vice versa, there was now just a huge gaping hole.

"Where are the escalators?" asked Eddie. "*Where are they?* Who steals escalators?"

All around the opening in the floor was old and torn caution tape, most of which lay on the dusty floor.

"This is bad…"said Kayla.

"Real bad," added Eddie as he angrily kicked pieces of broken floor tile into the dark void.

"Come on, let's get on the other side of the hole, so we can keep an eye on the zombies," said Cole as he rushed to the other side of the dark abyss. He didn't want the zombies to sneak up on them.

"So what now?" asked Eddie, looking down into the darkness in the floor where the escalators used to be. "Can we climb down?"

Eddie shone his light into the darkness and moved it around, looking for a way to get down there.

"***Arghhhh!***" he screamed, jumping back and tripping on some of the caution tape laying on the dirty floor.

. . .

"What now?!" asked Cole, exasperated, rushing over to Eddie's side.
Cole leaned over the dark hole and shone his flashlight below.
"Oh...," he whispered.
"Uh huh," muttered Eddie, stepping back from the dark hole in the floor.
"What?! *What is it?*" asked Kayla nervously.
"Take a look," said Cole quietly.
Kayla didn't like how Cole had said that.
She quickly turned her light down towards the bottom of the black opening.
A figure was standing on the bottom floor.
It was the Plague Doctor.
And he was looking up at the three friends.
"Jeeze!" shouted Kayla, jumping back from the opening. "That's freaky. How did he know we'd be here?"
"What the heck is going on?" asked Eddie. "Who *is* that guy? I feel like we're in some horror movie and any minute that freak with the mask is going to catch us and kill us."
"I don't know what that guy's deal is," said Cole. "But we've got a bunch of zombies inside the store coming to get us and we need to deal with that first."
"How is he controlling the zombies?" asked Kayla.
"I don't know. I can't explain any of this," answered Cole quietly. "None of this is making any sense."
"If we can't get down here we have to try and get to the other end of the mall, there should be a JC Penneys or something." said Kayla. "We're quickly running out of options here."
"What if it's boarded up too?" asked Eddie, with a worried and fearful expression on his face. "What then?"
"We'll deal with it when we get there," said Kayla, matter of factly. "But now we need to *go!*"
"We'll have to run past the zombies that are inside this store and get back

outside into the mall again," said Cole. "Let's go!"

The three were about to take off running when a zombie appeared from around one of the columns in front of Kayla. She let out a shriek and stumbled back, bumping into Eddie who grabbed her and kept her from falling down.

Cole turned and got behind the zombie and slammed into it's back, pushing it forward. The zombie stumbled, tripping and almost falling down. Cole rammed into the zombie one more time and this time Kayla stuck her foot out, tripping the zombie. The zombie lurched forward, falling towards the floor. Eddie ran up and gave it a good hard shove, sending it flailing over the edge of the gaping black hole and crashing to the ground below.

"Take that!" Eddie yelled at the falling creature.

"I hope it landed on that mask wearing freak!" said Eddie as he turned back to face his friends.

"Good job!" said Kayla. "Now let's get out of here! Run to the far side of the store, out of the light and we can circle around the zombies. Follow the walls until we get back to the doors."

The three took off at a run, their flashlights bobbing up and down as they ran to the opposite side of the huge store. When they reached the wall they turned to the right and followed the wall until they met another wall. They turned right again and followed that wall until they reached the doors leading out to the mall.

Chapter 18

The three YouTubers slowed down when they reached the doors leading from inside the Macy's store to the inside of the mall and Cole slowly peered outside.

"I don't see anything," he said as he checked to the left and right of the entrance. "Let's go!"

"To the left!" instructed Kayla as the three rushed out of the Macys. "We have to find another two story department store."

The friends raced down the mall concourse, past a shoe store and a small clothing store that still had some of it's signs hanging on the walls, now stained and mildewed.

Just in front of the three was the central mall courtyard.

"Whoa...look at that," said Cole as he slowed down a little and pointed to the lower level.

A large group of zombies were making their way towards the escalators.

"Oh crap," said Eddie dishearteningly.

"It gets worse," said Kayla quietly.

"Of course it does," Eddie mumbled, shaking his head.

On the second level, above the courtyard were elevated walkways that connected both sides of the upper level of the mall. Both of these crossings had zombies on them, coming directly towards the three explorers.

"We're right in the middle, guys!" said Eddie with alarm.

Cole was looking around, trying to find a way out.

"Guys?!" Eddie said with growing panic, "They're heading this way!"

Directly to the left of the three was a dark hallway located between two empty stores.

"Down there," said Cole, motioning towards the dark corridor.

"What?!" said Eddie. "Down the scary dark hallway? *Are you crazy?* We have no idea where it goes?"

"We're kind of out of options here," said Kayla, watching the zombies getting closer to them. "It probably leads to bathrooms or offices."

"I don't want to get trapped in the bathrooms!" exclaimed Eddie.

"Or," Cole said, "it leads to the hallways that connect to the back of the stores. The hallways the employees use. The service corridor."

"And what if it doesn't and we get trapped down there?" said Eddie.

"It won't," said Cole, "I've been in plenty of malls, I'm 99% certain this will lead to the service corridor."

"Well we don't have any other choice," said Kayla as she warily watched the zombies advancing on their position. "It's either down the dark, foreboding hallway or we fight past the zombies."

The zombies were now across the connecting walkways and were coming towards the three, in front and in back.

"OK guys, times up, we have to make a move," said Kayla, slowly walking towards the hallway, keeping her eyes on the zombies heading towards them. She could hear them growling and hissing.

Cole turned towards the hallway and jogged into the darkness, using his flashlight to light a path for him to see.

No one said a word as the three ran to the end of the hall. The paint on the walls of the hallway was peeling and some of the ceiling tiles had fallen and were laying scattered on the floor. There was various types of trash piled up along the bottom of the walls.

At the end, the hall turned to the right and the three followed the turn in the hall. The hallway continued but along the right side, every 20 or 30 feet was a door with a store's name painted on it. Each door led to one of the stores inside the mall.

"Yes!" exclaimed Cole with joy. "*I knew it!* Service corridor."

"Now let's just hope one of these is unlocked," he said hopefully.

Eddie let out a loud groan.

Kayla rushed up to the first door and tried the handle.

It was locked.

Eddie ran back to the corner of the hallway and peaked around the side. He could see several zombies walking around in the mall outside the hallway.

He ran back to join Cole and Kayla.

"The zombies are outside in the mall, but they haven't come down the hall yet."

Cole was at the second door, twisting the handle.

"It's locked," he said with disappointment, panic starting to rise in his voice.

Kayla looked at Eddie, they were both growing increasingly nervous. Eddie was tense with dread, *I think I might throw up*, he thought to himself, holding his stomach and trying to calm his nerves.

There were two more doors further down the corridor and then it looked like the hallway ended. Cole ran over to the third door and tried the handle.

It opened.

"Yes!" said Kayla and Eddie in unison, as Cole let out a sigh of relief.

Cole opened the door slowly and shined his light inside. Kayla ran over to the door, waving at Eddie. "Come on!" she shouted at him.

"Hang on," said Eddie as he turned and ran back to the corner of the hallway.

He slowly peaked around the corner.

"**Arghhh!**" he screamed as he came face to face with a zombie.

The zombie, only two feet away, growled loudly and swiped at Eddie with it's hand. The zombie's fingernails grazed Eddie's forehead, leaving several bleeding scratches.

Eddie recoiled in horror, "They're here!" he shouted. He ran his hand over his face, wiping blood away as he spun around and raced back to join Kayla and Cole.

Cole was holding the door open for him. As soon as Eddie was inside he slammed the door shut.

"Made it," said Eddie, leaning against the metal door, breathing hard and wiping blood from his forehead.

BAM
BAM
BAM

"Just barely," said Kayla shaking her head with relief.

The zombies had reached the door and were pounding on it from the other side.

Chapter 19

"We need to block the door!" said Cole, as he and Eddie leaned against it. "Kayla, try and find something we can prop up against the door."
Kayla quickly spun around and scanned the empty store with her flashlight.
"I see some display racks!" she shouted hopefully, rushing over to the left wall where there were several large wooden display racks stacked up in a pile. She grabbed one and pulled it towards the door. It was heavy and it took a lot of effort to drag it across the floor.
BAM
BAM
BAM
The zombies were still hitting the door, trying to push it open.
When Kayla got close to the door, Eddie moved out of the way and helped her push the wooden rack against part of the door. Once they got it against the door, Cole jumped out of the way and they slid it all the way in front of the door.
BAM
BAM
BAM
The pounding continued but the door barely budged.
"That worked out," said Eddie with relief.
"Yeah," said Cole with a sigh, "about time we caught a break."
The zombies were continuing to bang on the outside of the door.
"That won't hold forever," said Cole. "Let's get another one."
The three hurriedly went over to the pile of display racks and between the three of them managed to drag another two over to the door. They pushed them up against the other rack, forming a small pile.
"That should hold for a bit," said Eddie, breathing deeply and wiping blood

from the scratches on his forehead.

"We need weapons, *now*," said Kayla. "While we have a minute, look around and see what you can find in here."

"And hurry, before those zombies get smart and come around to the front of the store," said Cole, looking with concern towards the far end of the store.

The three friends dispersed throughout the store, using their flashlights to search for anything that they could possibly use as a weapon.

Cole found a metal clothing rack and managed to twist off the top of the metal stand. He then picked up the long metal pole and swung it experimentally.

This will do, he said to himself with a grin.

During Kayla's exploration of the empty store she found a fire extinguisher in a dusty corner. Someone had already used all the fire retardent but she could still use it as a club. She picked it up and joined Cole as they hurried over to where Eddie was to see how he was doing.

"I can't find anything!" he said with desperation, frantically searching along one wall with his light.

Kayla and Cole split up and scoured the store, trying to see if they could find something for Eddie to use as a weapon.

"Over here!" Kayla shouted. She was holding up a wooden stool that was missing one of the legs. She smashed the stool on the ground repeatedly until one of the two remaining legs broke free.

She held the broken leg up for Eddie.

"Now you have a spear, club thing," she said, smiling.

"Thanks," said Eddie. He took the stool leg from Kayla and gave it a few swings.

"Now we can get out here," Cole said.

BAM

BAM

BAM

The zombies were still banging on the door and it was only a matter of time before they would manage to push the wooden displays away from the door and get inside.

"We need to hurry and get through this store and back to the mall," said

Kayla as she hurried forward in the dark store, her flashlight lighting a path in front of them while she held onto the fire extinguisher with the other hand. Cole was behind her, and he had taken his camera out and was filming while he carried the large metal pole in his other hand. Lastly Eddie brought up the rear, keeping an eye on the blocked door behind them.

Chapter 20

The front of the store had it's security gate down and locked but on both sides the display windows were busted out.

Kayla hesitantly and slowly poked her head out of the busted right side window, holding her fire extinguisher up in case she encountered a zombie.

She looked around the outside of the store, then retreated back inside.

"All clear," she said, turning to Cole and Eddie. "I don't see any zombies."

"OK, so the plan is to keep going down the mall, towards the other end?" asked Eddie.

"Yep," said Cole, "no other choice."

"Ready?" asked Kayla, glancing towards the broken window.

"Let's go," said Cole, taking the lead and stepping through the broken window and out of the store -

Bumping right into a zombie.

"*Holy-!*" he managed to stutter before stumbling back inside the store as the zombie swung it's fist at Cole's face, spit flying from it's growling and gnashing mouth.

The swing missed, bust just barely.

"You said there weren't any zombies!" yelled Cole, backtracking into the store.

"There weren't!' said Kayla, pushing past him and jumping out of the store window. As she was landing, she swung her fire extinguisher at the zombie, smashing it in the head and knocking it to the ground.

"Hurry!" she shouted, kicking the zombie in the stomach and then taking off at a run. "Let's go!"

Cole and Eddie followed right behind her, avoiding the zombie laying on the floor. It hissed at them as they passed and tried to grab their legs.

Three more zombies had just come back down out of the hallway and were coming around the corner, approaching the front of the store.

Kayla and her three friends took off running down the mall.

"Whoa. We just barely made it out of there in time," said Eddie, looking back at the zombies.

The three hurried down the mall, far outpacing the slower zombies that were following them.

Eddie looked behind them again, there were several more zombies coming up the escalators and a lot more zombies were on the upper level and starting to spread out in different directions.

"This is insane," muttered Eddie. "You think this is happening everywhere?"

Kayla shook her head, "No...they only seem to be following that plague doctor guy. And for some reason they're in this mall."

"Yeah," moaned Eddie, "the same day we decided to come here. What are the odds of that? We finally get to explore the Linwood Mall and it gets overrun by zombies."

"I know, isn't it great?!" said Cole with a fake smile, trying to bring some levity to the situation. Kayla merely snorted at him and Eddie gave him a very mean look.

"Allright, just kidding. Let's keep moving before we get surrounded again," said Cole.

"Too late," said Kayla with dismay.

. . .

"*No!*" Eddie shouted angrily. "Not again!"

Not only were there four zombies chasing them, now there were another two zombies approaching them from the front.

Kayla shook her head, "They're not making this easy for us."

"Well," said Cole, putting his camera back inside his backpack, "we have to get past those two or else we're going to be trapped."

Cole grabbed his metal clothing rack pole with both hands and started jogging towards the zombies in front of the trio.

One of the zombies was a few steps ahead of its companion and it started to growl as Cole got closer to it. Cole closed the gap between himself and the zombie and with a loud yell he swung the metal pole at the zombies head, smashing into it and sending the zombie crashing to the floor.

The second zombie lunged at Cole.

Cole twisted to the side, trying to avoid the creature but it managed to grab onto his arm. Cole let out a yell and tried to shake the zombie free. It didn't work so he dropped his metal pole and started punching the zombies arm, and kicking at the zombie with his feet. The zombie snarled at him, and swiped at him with it's free hand.

Kayla had ran over to help Cole and she swung her fire extinguisher at the zombie, smashing it in the face. It immediately let go of Cole and stumbled backwards. Cole picked up his pole and stepped towards the zombie, swinging at it and striking it in the head. The zombie collapsed on the ground.

"Look out!" yelled Eddie coming up behind Cole and Kayla.

The first zombie Cole had knocked down had gotten back up and was about to attack the pair. Eddie ran up and swung his stool leg like a bat, smacking it in the face. The zombie wobbled sideways.

"Run!" Eddie shouted, racing past the two stunned zombies as Cole and Kayla quickly followed.

. . .

The three continued to run down the mall, avoiding the many puddles of water and other debris scattered across the tiled floor.

Behind them, the zombies still followed, growing in numbers.

Cole slowed down and took a quick look behind them. The zombies were still trailing them. He took a count of the zombies; the two they had fought past, the three from the service corridor, plus another ten or so were following those five.

"Fifteen zombies," Cole said, turning back around and jogging to catch back up with Eddie and Kayla.

"Great," moaned Eddie, "just great."

"We've got a lot of zombies coming after us. We need to get to that department store, like *now!*" Cole continued.

"What happens if that store is boarded up too?" asked Eddie nervously.

"We haven't had much luck with the big stores."

"We're toast," Cole answered without cracking a smile.

"If we get there and it's boarded up we'll be trapped by a horde of angry zombies." Kayla said. "There's no way we can fight that many."

Eddie wiped blood from the scratch across his forehead, "Maybe we should come up with a backup plan. Sure you guys don't want to hide somewhere?"

"There's nowhere to hide that those things won't see us or find us," said Cole sadly.

The trio passed several more empty stores on their journey to the big department store located at the end of the mall.

"Hey!" shouted Kayla as she stopped running and pointed excitedly at the opposite side of the mall. "The movie theater!"

Across from the three friends, tucked back from the main concourse was an old multi level movie theater.

"It's two stories!" said Eddie, jumping up and down. "Yes!"

"Let's get over there and take a look!" said Cole, "Great thinking Kayla!"

Eddie looked behind them, the zombies were still behind them and getting closer.

"We either have to go further down the mall to the next walkway that crosses over to the other side or run back to the last cross-over we passed." said Eddie anxiously. "Which one is better?"

"If we go forward and crossover, there's a chance the zombies could spread out behind us and crossover too, then we'd be trapped. If we double back we're running right towards them but as long as we make it to the crossway before them we're golden," explained Kayla.

"We just have to beat the zombies to the crossover," said Eddie with a frown.

"We can do it," said Cole.

"We *have* to do it," said Kayla seriously. "But we need to get going *now!*"

. . .

The trio turned around and ran back down the mall, in the direction they had just come from, heading straight towards the group of angry zombies.

When the zombies saw them they got excited and agitated. They snarled and gnashed their teeth while swiping the arms into the air.

"This better work," said Eddie nervously as he watched the zombies getting closer and closer as they ran towards them.

The elevated walkway that connected both sides of the mall was between the humans and the zombies and both groups were getting really close to it.

"Looks like we'll get there first!" said Cole assertively, relief evident in his voice.

We'd better, thought Eddie worriedly, *we'd better*.

"Almost there!" said Kayla smiling excitedly as they neared the crossover.

The zombies were almost there too.

"It's going to be close!" said Eddie, his eyes darting back and forth from the walkway to the zombies.

The zombies were getting closer and their growling and hissing was louder.

The two groups were now only a few feet apart.

"These guys stink!" gasped Eddie, wrinkling his nose in disgust.

The three kept running and it appeared that they were going to run right into the group of zombies. But at the last second, Cole made a hard left turn and ran down the elevated walkway, Kayla and Eddie right behind him.

"Yes!" said Cole. "We made it!"

The two zombies in front of the pack reached out just as Kayla was running past them, swiping at her with their bony hands and dirty fingernails.

"**Arrgh!**" she shouted as one of the zombies scratched up her arm and across her neck.

"You OK?" asked Eddie with alarm.

Kayla nodded and kept running, wiping the blood from her neck without ever slowing down.

"That was close!" said Eddie as he ran beside her.

"You're telling me."

The zombies hadn't expected the trio to turn and run down the elevated walkway and it took a moment for them to realize what had happened and change their own course to follow after them.

Cole continued to lead the way as the three ran across the walkway until they reached the other side.

Chapter 21

To the right of the crossover, sitting back about 50 feet from the main thoroughfare was an abandoned two-level movie theater.
Cole passed two closed up stores as he led the trio closer to the theater.
"*Yes!*" he shouted over his shoulder at his friends. "I see the escalators!"
Kayla let out a sigh of relief as Eddie shouted with joy.
The theater had its own set of escalators, going up and down from the upper level screening rooms to the screening rooms on the lower level. Each floor also had its own small lobby and concession stand.
Kayla noticed the old movie posters for *Harry Potter and the Goblet of Fire* and *Zathura*, still in their glass cases mounted on the lobby walls.
Just as they reached the first escalator, Eddie turned to look behind them.
The zombies were only about fifteen feet behind them.
"They're here!" he shouted with alarm.

. . .

"Get down the escalators!" yelled Cole, as the three friends raced towards the escalators that let from the second floor of the movie theater down to the ground level.
"They're behind us, hurry!" shouted Eddie with panic and fear.
Kayla was the first to reach the escalators, "There are zombies coming up the escalators!" she shouted, slowing down when she reached the top steps.
A pair of zombies were beginning to ascend the escalators.
Eddie pushed past Kayla and started to go down the steps of the escalator, "We have to go down, there are too many zombies up here!"
Kayla and Cole followed Eddie and started to descend the steps with the large group of zombies only a few feet behind them and closing

in.

"*Go!*" shouted Cole as he pushed Kayla and Eddie forward.

Cole turned around and swung his metal pole at the zombies that were nearest him. They snarled and lurched back, barely managing to stay out of range of the weapon.

The two zombies climbing up the steps from the ground floor were getting closer and closer to Eddie.

Eddie let out a primal scream, "**Arghh!**" and stepped closer to the zombie in front, swinging his stool leg at the zombie and smashing it in the face.

The zombie slid sideways but before Eddie had a chance to get past it the second zombie stepped up to fill the open space.

"Dang it!" shouted Eddie in frustration, swinging his make-shift bat at the zombie in front of him. The zombie dodged the swing and swung it's fist at Eddie. It wasn't close enough to make contact but Eddie stepped back just in case. The first zombie had recovered from it's hit and also swung a punch at Eddie. Eddie was forced to take another step backwards and bumped into Kayla.

Behind them Cole was swinging his metal staff at any zombie that got too close to him but more and more zombies were coming down the escalator and they were pushing against each other and getting closer and closer to Cole, forcing him to keep going down the steps.

"Guys!" Cole shouted over his shoulder, "*Move!* There's too many up here!"

"Go!" Kayle yelled at Eddie, pushing his shoulder forward.

"I can't! There's two of them and my toothpick isn't doing any good!" hollered Eddie loudly and angrily.

"Move over," said Kayla, pushing past Eddie as he slid beside her. She hefted her fire extinguisher up and swung it hard at the nearest zombie, making direct contact with its face. Blood splattered in the air and the zombie fell backward into the zombie behind it.

Kayla stepped forward and hit the zombie again and again, forcing the two zombies down the escalator. Eventually the first zombie collapsed on the steps and stopped moving. Kayla then turned her rage onto the remaining zombie and attacked it, forcing it to back up under the onslaught of her swings. After several direct blows to the head, the zombie also collapsed on the steps.

Kayla stepped over the zombie, took three more steps and then she was off of the escalator and standing on the mall floor.

"Nice!" said Eddie with relief and admiration as he buried to join her on the ground floor. He turned to yell back up to Cole, "Cole! Come on!"

Kayla and Eddie took up defensive positions at the base of the escalators in case any more zombies appeared.

Up on the escalator Cole was busy fighting off the mob of zombies that were getting too close to him but more and more were crowding down the escalators, pushing the horde closer and closer to Cole.

"Run!" shouted Kayla.

She wanted to go up and help Cole but there wasn't enough room and she'd only end up getting in the way, blocking his escape.

Cole took one more swing with his metal pole and then turned to run down the escalator steps. He managed to take one step before the mass of zombies pushing down the escalators swarmed over him.

"*No!*" screamed Kayla, as she watched her friend disappear under the mob of angry zombies. Eddie's mouth dropped open in horror and his wooden stool leg dropped out of his hand and clattered along the tiled floor.

Cole was completely covered by the mob of zombies.

"No, no, no…" mumbled Kayla. She thought about going to help but there were too many zombies and there was no way she could fight them all off.

Eddie dropped to the floor, sobbing violently into his hands.

Kayla burst into tears, turning away from the snarling, group of zombies that were kicking and punching each other, trying to get to Cole.

Rage filled Kayla and she turned back to the escalators and began to advance up the steps, blinded by hatred and sadness. She gripped the fire extinguisher tightly in her hand as she made her way up the steps.

"What are you doing?!" shrieked Eddie, getting up off of the floor. He could barely see her through the tears streaming down his face. "*We have to go!*"

Kayla didn't hear Eddie, all she could think of was killing every single zombie on the escalators.

"Kayla!" Eddie shouted as loud as he could. "*Kayla!*"

Kayla finally stopped climbing up the steps.

"We have to go!" pleaded Eddie, eyes filled with tears.

The zombies had finished with Cole and turned their attention to Kayla and Eddie.

Kayla turned around and hurried back down the steps to where Eddie was waiting for her at the bottom.

She passed Eddie, without saying a word, her eyes filled with pain and tears as she focused straight ahead.

The two ran away from the movie theater escalators, down the dark hallway that led out into the main mall thoroughfare.

"I don't see any zombies," said Eddie cautiously.

Kaylay didn't respond, she just kept moving forward.

"I can see the mall, we're almost there," said Eddie, with relief as they approached the main mall floor. "Then we can get the heck out of here and let the cops kill all these-"

"**ARGGHHH!!**"

. . .

Just as Eddie and Kayla were about to step out into the main mall concourse, a figure came around the corner in front of them, blocking their path.

It was the Plague Doctor.

"*What?!*" Kayla managed to stammer as she stumbled away from the masked person.

Eddie froze in shock, "How…?"

The Plague Doctor reached out and grabbed his wrist.

"Hey!" Eddie shouted, jerking his wrist free from the doctor's grasp and staggering back a few steps.

Kayla watched in horror as Eddie took one more step backwards and then collapsed on the floor.

"*Eddie!*" she screamed, dropping the fire extinguisher and running over to him.

She knelt beside him, and shook him, "Eddie!" she cried.

Eddie didn't move.

"*What did you do!*" she hollered with rage as she fixed her eyes on the doctor.

"I released him," the Plague Doctor said in a calm voice.

"*What!?*" Kayla screamed. "What are you talking about?! *What did you do?*"

"Calm yourself," the doctor continued, in his quiet and calculated voice, "I healed him and set him free."

"*I'll set you free!*" Kayla screamed at him. She bent down and picked up the fire extinguisher and lifted it in the air.

The doctor just stood there, calmly watching her.

As Kayla stood facing the doctor, she released a string of profanity at him. Behind the doctor, the zombies were walking up. When they reached the doctor they stood behind him, waiting.

The doctor continued, "It's been quite an interesting day but now it must end." The doctor looked down at Eddie's body, "I have more work to attend to."

Kayla looked behind the zombies and saw Cole's lifeless body laying in a huge pool of blood on the escalator. She looked down and saw Eddie lying still at her feet.

Sobbing, she turned to face the doctor again. "What do you want?" she asked, angry, tired and shocked by what was unfolding around her.

"I want to heal the world," the doctor answered, "purge the planet of-"

"*I don't care!*" Kayla interrupted with a scream and threw the fire extinguisher at the Plague Doctor. He tried to dodge it but it hit him in the chest, knocking him backwards. As soon as she threw the extinguisher Kayla broke into a run and dashed past the doctor and out into the mall.

A zombie stepped in front of her but she elbowed it aside roughly, pushing past it as she ran on.

She never looked back, running towards the service corridor she and her friends had used to get inside the mall.

"Get her!" she heard the doctor yell, but she didn't turn around to see, she just kept running.

The zombies chased after her but they were far too slow. Kayla was running on pure adrenaline and wasn't about to slow down.

She ran on, as fast as she could, jumping over boxes and piles of trash.

Up ahead, she could see some of the familiar stores that they had seen when they'd first entered the mall.

Yes! She thought with joy when she reached the corridor that the trio had used to gain access to the mall.

Kayla ran down the hallway, avoiding the puddles of water until she arrived at the dirty and grimy maintenance room at the end. She rushed over to the boarded up door, got down and crawled over the broken glass and out of the small opening between the door frame and the plywood nailed to the outside.

When she was clear of the door she stood up outside…

… and collided with a figure dressed all in black.

. . .

Kayla let out a horrible scream and swung her fists at the figure. The figure in front of her easily avoided the punch and swatted her hand away. Kayla stumbled back in shock and took a second to focus on the thing in front of her.

It was *not* the Plague Doctor.

It was a person wearing all black tactical SWAT gear, including a helmet, body armor, boots, a knife, pistol and an MP5 machine gun. She then noticed the large group of similarly dressed SWAT members standing behind the soldier in front of her.

I'm safe! she thought, as tears of joy streamed down her face.

"You need to come with us," said the soldier in front of Kayla.

Before Kayla could say anything or move two soldiers stepped around the lead soldier and grabbed her.

"Hey!" she yelled, twisting and struggling, trying to break free. The soldiers were too strong and she couldn't get loose. Another soldier walked up and injected something into her arm with a needle.

Kayla screamed at them and then everything went black.

Chapter 22

The soldiers that Kayla ran into outside the mall are part of an elite security force called the *Mobile Task Force* that work for the facility that the Plague Doctor escaped from.
These soldiers had been tracking the doctor since the moment he escaped. They had been closing in on him but it wasn't until they intercepted a distress call to the local police department that they were finally able to pinpoint his exact location. The call they intercepted was about a group of angry people at an abandoned mall that just so happened to be a few miles from where the soldiers were currently searching. They immediately wrapped up at that location and headed for the Linwood Mall.

With a force of over twenty soldiers, they entered the mall at the same spot Kayla and her friends had. There was another contingent of soldiers in blacked-out SUVs patrolling the perimeter of the mall in case anyone or anything managed to sneak past the soldiers inside the mall.
Once inside the mall, the soldiers spread out and advanced through the lower level, searching the entire floor and every store.
It didn't take long to locate the doctor and his zombies and capturing the Plague Doctor was relatively easy. The Plague Doctor was casually sitting next to the body of a young man dressed in all black. A large mob of zombies were standing around the doctor.
The doctor was performing surgery on the corpse when the soldiers arrived.
The Plague Doctor looked up as the men approached him but before he could even say a word they shot him with several tranquilizer darts, knocking him out cold. As for the young man laying on the floor, they put a bullet in his head, making sure he would not come back as a zombie.
Almost simultaneously the soldiers began shooting all the zombies

that were around the doctor. And they didn't stop until there were no more zombies left standing.

Four soldiers then tied the doctor up. All the soldiers wore gloves and had on long sleeved uniforms and took every precaution to make sure none of their skin made contact with the doctor. Once he was properly restrained, the soldiers hauled the doctor out of the mall and loaded him into a waiting SUV that promptly departed.

Then the soldiers searched the entire mall, making sure every zombie was accounted for and killed. Each zombie was then put into a black body bag and taken out of the mall and loaded up in a waiting van. The bodies of Eddie and Cole were also collected, bagged, and removed.

After all that was done a separate team entered the mall and made sure all blood and any other traces of human and zombie were removed and wiped clean.

Then they set the mall on fire.

. . .

That night on the 10 o'clock news the news anchor reported this lead story:

"Today around 6:00, witnesses reported seeing smoke coming from the old Linwood Mall. Firefighters arrived at the scene and reported seeing the entire mall engulfed in flames. Police cordoned off the area for several blocks while the fire department tried to control the fire.

The Fire Chief said that he had never seen a building burn so fast and so quickly; especially one that size. There wasn't much they could do and had to just let the fire burn itself out.

Several empty buildings that shared the mall parking lot also caught fire and burned to the ground.

Next to the Linwood Mall was the Brighton Leadership Academy which was also engulfed in flames. The academy is a center for alternative college courses.

We're also getting reports that there may be students inside the building.

We'll keep you posted."

Then at the end of the 10 o'clock news that same night this was reported:

"We are saddened and horrified to report the deaths of 27 students and 2 employees of the Brighton Leadership Academy. According to the Fire Chief, for some reason they were all trapped inside the Academy and died in the fire. Preliminary investigation suggests that they may have been overwhelmed with toxic fumes from the burning building and passed out before they could escape the fire. The community is heartbroken over this loss of life and such wonderful potential.

The Fire Chief went on to say that due to the intense heat of the fire, no bodies were able to be recovered. Sadly everyone inside was cremated.

This is truly a sad and horrible day."

Epilogue

Kayla slowly opened her eyes.
She could feel herself starting to become aware and cognizant.
There was so much light in the room.
Why is it so bright? She wondered.
Her clouded mind began to focus more.
Huh...where am I?
She turned her head to the side. She was in her apartment, laying on the couch.

She sat up slowly and quickly grabbed her head with her hands; her head was throbbing and she had a horrible headache.
Why am I on the couch? She thought, grimacing with pain.
Kayla never slept on the couch.
She looked down and noticed she was wearing jeans and her favorite blue sweatshirt. Both were very dirty and covered with stains and smudges.
What? She struggled to try and remember why she had slept on the couch in her dirty clothes.
For some reason she couldn't remember anything.
How did she get so dirty?

She thought harder and the last thing she could remember was going to the grocery store Wednesday afternoon for some snacks and then coming home and charging up her phone before she started to do some reading about the Linwood Mall. She couldn't remember anything after that.
She noticed her cell phone laying on the coffee table in front of the couch. She picked it up and turned it on. The home screen said Saturday, 10AM.
What? Saturday?!
Kayla was starting to panic, the last thing she remembered was Wednesday!
Why can't I remember Thursday or Friday?

She quickly texted her two friends, Cole and Eddie. The three were supposed to explore the old mall on Friday, the Friday she couldn't remember.
She sent the text and waited.
And waited.
They usually answer pretty quickly, she thought with concern.
She continued to wait.
Then she noticed her phone had several voicemails.
She listened to them.
Her mom had called five times to say how sorry she was about the death of her two friends and ask if she was OK.
What?!
Kayla said in stunned silence.
She replayed the voicemails.
According to her mom's message, Eddie and Cole had both died in a car wreck.
Both of them.
She couldn't wrap her mind around what she'd heard.
She listened to the voicemail again.
And again.
She remembered talking to the guys about their plan to explore the mall and they were all going to scout it out but that was all she could recall.
Why can't I remember anything?!
No way she thought, this must be a mistake.
She flipped through the pics on her phone. There were no new pics after Wednesday.
What? How can that be? Today is Saturday... How can I be missing two days?
Kayla started to panic, *What happened on Thursday and Friday?*
She called her mom. Her mom told her what she'd heard about the car wreck on the news.
According to her mom, Eddie and Cole had gotten into a wreck friday night. They ran off the road and hit a tree, the car caught fire and they died.
Kayla cried and cried.
Her mom tried to console her as best she could and she was alarmed at

Kayla's memory loss and thought someone had drugged her.

But who? And why?

The last thing Kayla remembered was researching the mall at home, alone on Wednesday night.

The two were puzzled and worried.

When her mom told her about the fire at the mall Kayla almost dropped the phone.

"It burned down?" she'd asked her mother in bewilderment. "The Linwood Mall?"

"Yes. Friday night, and some other buildings too. In fact one was a small college prep school and all 27 people inside died in the fire. It's horrible, just horrible." her mom had said sadly.

"And that's the same day as Cole and Eddie's car wreck?" asked Kayla slowly.

"Yes."

No way.

Something didn't feel right to Kayla.

There was definitely something up.

First her amnesia, her two best friends die in a car wreck and burn up, and then the mall they were supposed to explore burns to the ground. And all this happens on the same day?

Nope, No way.

If only I could remember!

The frustration was driving Kayla insane.

Her mom suggested they go see a doctor and maybe they can determine if she was drugged or if not why she had amnesia. Maybe they could get some of her memories back.

And then Kayla could discover what really happened on Friday...

THE END

Thank you for reading.

More of my work can be seen at:
Ctupa.com

Instagram: artofctupa

Christopher Tupa
christophertupa@hotmail.com

Printed in Great Britain
by Amazon